THE LIES THEY TOLD

JAY NADAL

Published by 282publishing.com

1

THE DESIRE for revenge gnawed away inside Dean Macholl like a rat. A giant sewer rat with sharp, pointy teeth. Relentless and unceasing, it had consumed his thoughts for the past five years. His thirst for vengeance festered like a septic wound, and the only effective remedy was cold hard retribution.

This was about settling old scores.

An unnecessary flight delay infuriated him further. Usually, the short flight from Belgium back to London Heathrow took just over an hour, but he still sat waiting in departures. To pass the time, he watched the suits, as he liked to call business people, scurrying to the departure gates. Children sat quietly with their parents, consumed with a Netflix film, or a computer game.

How different his life had been. Dean could just imagine parents placing a protective arm around their kids and coaxing them away from him if they knew he'd spent years locked behind bars.

Once onboard, he gazed out of the small window to his right as the grey blanket of clouds masked the world below. His mind drifted back to his incarceration. Surrounded by four grubby white walls, there was nothing to do but stare at them for twenty-three hours a day. The paint had started to chip off with the passage of time or abuse by other prisoners.

If they think UK prisons are a shithole, then they need to spend time in a Belgian prison. It was well documented that many Belgian prisons had difficult and inhumane conditions. Cells and toilets were not cleaned, nor was rubbish removed. Many on the outside would argue *if you do the crime, you do the time*, so he hadn't expected sympathy. But it didn't stop the haunting memories of abuse, torture and murders he had witnessed on the inside. If the system didn't get you physically, it would break you psychologically. Many escaped by taking their own lives.

Dean had imagined life beyond the barbed wire since the first day of his sentence. Now he was free, it felt surreal. The luxury of stepping outside to his local to enjoy a pint or stopping off at his local chippy to get cod and chips. Simple pleasures he could now experience.

The air stewardess trundled down the aisle, pushing her drinks trolley, glancing from side to side, repeating the same line she had said a thousand times. The bottles clinked and rattled as she came alongside him.

"Anything to drink, sir?" she asked.

Five years without a drink. He swallowed hard as his mouth moistened at the prospect of having his first drink. Spoiled for choice, he left the stewardess waiting as he considered his options.

"Whisky, two bottles of whisky," he murmured.

"And what mixers would you like, *sir*?" A tinge of frost laced her polite tone.

Macholl shook his head in response.

The stewardess sighed before passing the drinks across the seats and taking his money. She offered him a smile, false but courteous, before hurrying along the aisle.

He swirled the whisky in the plastic cup, listening to the chinking of the ice cubes, breathing in a fragrance only years in an oak barrel could achieve. Just watching its gentle vortex was hypnotising, an aged single malt. When the liquid settled, he brought it to his cracked lips and let the amber fluid sit in his mouth a short time before swallowing. He closed his eyes, dwelling only on the flavour. God it was good. It seared his throat on the way down.

By the second bottle, the whisky was having the desired effect, as his shoulders slumped, and his head rolled back into the seat. His thoughts turned to Jack Taylor, 'Beanie' to those who knew him. Life should have been so different. One hundred and fifty thousand pounds different, his share from their last job together. But Jack had screwed him over. It was the reason he'd gone on the run and fled the country. Short of money he had committed a string of robberies, the last of which had led to his capture and imprisonment.

He switched on the phone again and read the text message. A courier had delivered the phone to him in prison the day of his release. With no note attached, and no identifying marks on the brown jiffy bag, he had switched it on to discover one text message. A birthday celebration. Dean's lips stiffened as he read the message once again. *Is this Jack's way of apologising and mending bridges?* There were few who would have followed Dean's incarceration and his subsequent release. But he was sure Jack would have kept his ear to the ground, waiting for Dean's return.

Jack had had the nickname of 'Beanie' for as long as Dean could remember. From their early days of peddling drugs on street corners, and knifepoint street robberies, Jack had always worn a beanie hat regardless of the weather, come rain, snow or shine. As time went by, his associates referred to him as 'Beanie' rather than Jack.

Dean couldn't determine the reason behind the invitation. Jack was either brave, or stupid. He suspected the former. In all the time he had known Jack, the man wore his bravado like a cloak. Just holding his gaze for more than a second or two had often resulted in a blinding flash of anger.

Jack, a man to be feared. On their last job, an uncomfortable feeling had captured Dean's attention about Jack's behaviour and the way he looked at him. Jack had a cold, aggressive and menacing stare, where his eyes were void of all emotion and the colour would drain from his face. The same stare he wore moments before erupting in a fit of rage and violence. It was a split-second transformation offering his victim no time to escape. Dean had lost count of the number of people Jack had put in hospital, or an early grave.

The stare had been the precursor to Jack pulling the trigger.

A bullet had hit Elaine Atkins as she stood behind the counter of the bookies. As Jack's girlfriend, her role in the raid had been to disable the security system. Jack had spent months charming the woman. He'd lavished her with gifts, and taken her into his world of drinking and gambling dens, building society and security van raids, drug trafficking and extortion.

A smitten Elaine would do anything Jack asked of her. She adored his power, his wealth, his charm and his line of chat. Sadly, she'd been nothing more than an extra on his film set, unnoticed and unimportant.

Dean had reassured her she'd be okay.

Jack, Jack. Why did you have to ruin everything, you moron?

Anger flashed through Dean once again. They had been on a roll, growing their businesses and their reputations. But Jack became unhinged, and it was their eventual downfall.

Dean's thoughts were like a patchwork quilt, pieces that didn't fit together but somehow formed a shape. He had so many questions, he didn't know where to start.

It felt like they had just taken off when the captain announced they were beginning their descent into London Heathrow. He strapped himself back in as another air hostess weaved from side to side as she made her way up the aisle checking belts were fastened, and seats were in the upright position.

See you soon, 'Beanie', real soon.

HE LEFT THE PLANE, and took in deep breaths of air. British air. It felt good to be back. He made his way through passport control, the officer at the desk giving him a cursory look as he stared at Dean's picture. With short cropped greying hair, and an equally grey beard, there were distinguishing features missing from his passport photograph. He was also considerably thinner. His once tight leather jacket hung from his shoulders as if it belonged to someone else, and the belt on his jeans had been pulled in one extra notch. Dean stared back at the officer, keen to get through. Rules and regulations just incited his annoyance, along with people in uniform.

"There you go, sir. Have a good day," the officer said, sliding the passport through the gap in the glass shield.

The throng of people waiting in arrivals overwhelmed him. His heartbeat quickened, and his mouth dried. Having been stuck in a prison cell for five years, he wasn't used to being in a crowded space as he pushed his way through the milling travellers until he stepped on to the pavement. The smell of diesel oil, aviation fuel and cigarette smoke made his head spin.

He was home, had his freedom back and that felt good. He moved closer to where passengers huddled in a segregated area for smokers. They all stood looking at each other, aware of how antisocial their habit was. He tapped the Camel from his pack, and lit the end, the tobacco and paper sizzling in the flame. Inhaling, he let the nicotine hit every cell of his being, as he closed his eyes and savoured the moment.

Dean glanced around and looked for anyone who might be watching him from a distance. He looked for telltale signs like shifty eyes. A solitary male or female who looked out of place. He couldn't see anyone drawing attention.

In a way, he had hoped she would be there to greet him, to throw her arms around him. It was wishful thinking on his part. Despite having no sense of urgency in his actions, he felt uneasy. Having not had the opportunity for five years, it felt awkward to move, or to walk any considerable distance. And yet he found himself wanting to do just that. To take extra-long steps, and swing his arms like a child, just because he could.

Dean smiled at the thought. A phrase floated across his consciousness. One from prison he'd recited many times. Now he was free, he could say it out aloud. "One day I will hurt you. I promise. Your knife, my back. My gun, your head."

2

An unassuming and family-run Italian business provided the backdrop for the party. Tucked away in a quiet street in Holborn, Central London, it offered the discretion needed where "jobs" were discussed. Three post office raids, two security truck raids, the last being in Clerkenwell a few weeks ago, and the delivery of countless drugs, had been planned and agreed here. From the outside it looked like a typical Italian restaurant, with dark mood lighting, red and white checked tablecloths, hanging baskets of flowers, and Italian specials written in chalk on an A-frame blackboard.

Many Londoners who passed by wouldn't have noticed the two men loitering either side of the door. Thickset, and bald; one more muscular, the other carrying more than a few extra pounds around his waistline. They watched each car and taxi that cruised by. Each passer-by that came within a few inches of them, sparking their attention, stiffened their shoulders in a passive-aggressive way. Their job, to assess the risk to life of those they guarded. Those inside had more than their fair share of enemies, people they had double-crossed, crime families they had disrespected, and families they'd left in tatters.

"Are you sure they won't mind us coming?" Molly asked.

Harry placed a protective arm around her shoulder and pulled her in closer before placing a soft kiss on the top of her head. At six foot two, he towered over her by a foot. Topping the scales at thirteen stone, he looked powerful and athletic, and far older than his twenty years. Those characteristics had attracted her to him. She felt safe in his presence and protected when wrapped in his arms. He offered heart-warming relief to what she had been through in life. As clichéd as it was to say, Harry was her rock.

"Will you chillax? Ben invited us. And his mum is cool with that."

She rolled her bottom lip across her teeth in nervous anticipation. "Yeah, I know. You keep telling me that. But we don't really know them. Not really. Well, you do… And… But I don't. Besides…" Her voice trailed off as she made a hash of her words.

Harry laughed. "Listen, you know Ben, and you've met his mum. And to be honest, I won't know half the people there, either. I'm not messing, but you look cracking in that dress and I bet all eyes will be on you."

That's what she feared. For most of her life, eyes had been on her. Some welcomed, but many unwelcomed. Until meeting Harry, she had met few who had soft, caring and sensitive eyes. The majority had been cold, dark, menacing or lecherous. They had undressed her with their eyes, fantasising about what they would do to her.

With dark brown eyes and matching dark brown hair cascading midway down her back, she cast a striking image. She rarely wore make-up, which Harry loved. He kept reassuring her that her natural complexion and freckles made her look endearing. She had a slight frame, not through choice but circumstance and upbringing. She hid it well in the skintight black dress she wore this evening, its hem riding daringly high. Harry had struggled to keep his eye on the road as he stroked her soft, milky inner thigh. She had parted her legs in response, yearning his touch that sent shivers through her body. She had gasped as his fingers explored beneath her knickers, her reaction instant as she pushed back into the seat and moistened to his touch.

She wrapped her arms around her chest and stared at the pavement as they walked. Sensing her anxiety, he sought to reassure her further.

"Trust me; it will be fine. Besides you'll be sitting next to me. We turn up, have something to eat, and then make our excuses. The main thing is we show our faces. I think Ben would be pissed off if we didn't come. And to be honest, the birthday boy will love the attention, and he'll be splashing the cash, cigars, champagne, the whole works. Give it an hour and he'll be off his head, and then we can bugger off."

The restaurant appeared as they turned the corner. They were immediately drawn to the two henchmen positioned by the doorway. She cast a nervous eye in Harry's direction as he smiled at her with a reassuring wink.

"We are here for the party? Ben invited us."

Harry gave their names and waited while the men conferred and checked their phones, confirming they could proceed.

She pulled in closer to Harry as they stepped through the door. They were welcomed with a wall of warmth that bathed their faces. A waiter pointed towards the rear of the restaurant as they weaved between the tables. The familiar smell of pasta, pizzas and Italian herbs filled the air. There was a relaxed, cosy atmosphere in the restaurant, with low ceilings and subdued lighting.

They made their way towards what was referred to as the "backroom", a separate dining area often hired for private functions. It was a long, narrow room covering the width of the restaurant, with fixed, comfy seating to one wall, a row of tables, and individual chairs on the other side. Decorative pieces and oversized mirrors created a feeling of space and airiness.

The setting was so far removed from her own life that it felt alien to Molly. She often had nothing more than half a packet of Rich Tea biscuits for dinner, or a packet of Pom-Bear crisps for lunch. That's all they could afford. Occasionally, she had sneaked a few pound coins to treat herself to a bottle of Coke and a bar of chocolate.

As they reached the "backroom", the sounds from the front of the restaurant were drowned out by crass laughter. More than twenty people filled the room. Champagne bottles littered the table, and a heavy veil of smoke hung like a floating curtain a few feet above the tables. The strong smell of cigars attacked her throat and tickled her nostrils. She wanted to cough but suppressed it for fear of attracting further attention.

As they approached the tables, Ben pushed his chair back and made his way towards Harry.

"Yo, man, thanks for coming." Ben and Harry embraced like long-lost brothers, their handshake buried between them. And they were like brothers. Best friends since primary school, they had looked out for each other. They had shared similar interests and had grown up on neighbouring estates.

"Sorry we're a bit late. Molly couldn't do her hair at home, so she came back to mine. But then we got a bit sidetracked." Harry winked in Ben's direction, as Molly's face flushed crimson with embarrassment.

Ben turned towards Molly and welcomed her with a hug.

"You ain't half scrubbed up well," he remarked, his thick cockney accent sounded cheeky, as he looked her up and down.

Yet another man looking me up and down.

"No wonder you were late, mate."

The laddish banter did little to calm her nerves as they moved closer to the tables. Diane, Ben's mum, also rose to greet them and show them to their seats.

Jack gave them nothing more than a cursory look before he continued conversations with several men at one end of the table. With a glass of champagne in one hand, and a fat cigar in the other, his menacing stare and underlying wealth and power were matched by a large gold bracelet that hung loosely from his wrist and several gold rings stuffed on his chubby fingers.

Molly gripped Harry's hand under the table, squeezing it for reassurance.

Waiters placed out a large selection of dishes at random intervals along the table, and guests picked through them at leisure. Molly wasn't sure where to begin. All the foods were alien to her, and it took some coaxing from Harry before she forked some food on to her plate and enjoyed the new flavours that danced in her mouth. Her stomach growled in appreciation.

She sneaked a couple of glances in Jack's direction. He had a formidable reputation, and truth be told, he terrified her. The stories Harry had told her about Jack made him sound godlike in the criminal world. The men leant across the table, craning their necks and listening to every word that left his lips. None of them would win any awards in the good-looking category. Shaved heads, cropped hair, broken noses, and stubbly beards added to the aura of aggression that surrounded them.

Jack looked no better. With a Roman nose, and a greying beard to match his swept-back brown hair with a grey tint, he looked as if he'd been through the wringer. His face was round, his lips were thin, and his eyes were small. Seeing everything and revealing nothing. Even from this distance, she could hear his hard and deep voice.

Catching herself staring for too long, Molly glanced back at her food as Jack caught her eye. She dared not look up again, afraid just the strength of his intense gaze could terrify her further. This wasn't the first time she had seen him. Jack had been seen on the estate when he needed to sort a problem his foot soldiers hadn't managed to fix. Though he came mob-handed, he was more than comfortable turning up on his own. His reputation preceded him. But for his own safety, and fear of reprisals from other crime families, he would always take a few heavies for backup.

He had been on her estate not long ago, tearing up the place and looking for Finchy. For someone so loud and arrogant, Finchy had disappeared through the cracks in the pavement when Jack had arrived.

Darren Finch was her mum's boyfriend, in the loosest sense of the word, who also headed up the local crew on their estate. He ruled the estate with his fists, and he was no better behind closed doors. Finchy had intimidated her, and made her mum's life a misery.

3

SITTING no more than a few feet away from Jack, Molly suppressed a shiver. The man reduced Finchy to a snivelling coward when he had finally tracked him down. Surrounded on all four sides by apartments, Jack had dragged Finchy to the middle of the courtyard in an act of public humiliation. Jack pinned Finchy to the ground, before unleashing a torrent of violence as Finchy screamed for his life, his legs thrashing wildly, his hands pinned beneath Jack's legs, who sat astride him.

Jack stood and wiped the blood from his hands. If Finchy thought that the attack was over, he was wrong. The heavies took over, kicking the crumpled form until he moved no more. Finchy had stepped above his station, promising too much, taking even more, and spiralling into debt as he siphoned off profits for his own greed. Jack Taylor oversaw the drugs trade and Finchy was nothing more than a conduit, a supply line. And that's the way Jack preferred it. The more levels he put between him and the police, the less likely they were to find him at the head of the business.

Molly hoped Finchy would leave them alone, but she'd been sorely mistaken. Finchy had bounced back not long after.

"Are you okay, babe?" Harry asked, wiping his mouth the back of his hand.

"Yeah, I'm fine. Why?"

Harry shook his head. "Dunno. You look odd?"

Molly grimaced. "Oh, cheers. I love your compliments."

Harry backtracked. "I didn't mean it that way. It looks as if you're not enjoying yourself."

She wasn't. As much as she loved the food, and being with Harry, she'd rather not be at the party. It felt alien to her. She looked longingly in to his eyes. For the first time in her life, she was happy. With no close friends, and a broken family, she had no one to turn to. But Harry was there now, and only he knew the truth. Harry knew about Finchy's bullying and intimidation. He knew Molly's mum had been used as a drugs mule in return for a few wraps and a wad of cash. And he knew what was coming Molly's way if Finchy had anything to do with it. They could share in each other's pain. It was them against the world, or that's how she saw it anyway.

One minute Molly and Harry were deep in conversation, and the next, the atmosphere soured as tension prickled in the air.

"Well well, look what the cat dragged in," Jack growled. His eyes narrow and cold, the muscles in his jaws flexing and tightening as he stood and strode towards the opening where the man stood.

The men seated close to Jack pulled their shoulders back, their hands turning into clenched fists, ready to launch at a moment's notice.

"Someone invited me, Jack." Dean Macholl turned the screen of the mobile phone in Jack's direction. His eyes left Jack's face for a moment as they locked on to Diane, who had joined Jack's side. She stood with one arm wrapped across her chest, the other resting on it as she nibbled her nails. The confrontation frayed her nerves, stealing the moisture from her mouth, and widening her eyes underneath the force of her fear.

"Hello, Diane," Macholl said, his eyes not leaving her.

"I didn't give you permission to talk to my missus. In fact, I didn't give you permission to come here in the first place. Is it some kind of wind-up?" he snarled.

Macholl smiled to himself. He could read Jack easily.

"My guess is you're wondering how I got past your two meatheads. Well you hadn't considered the kitchen has its own rear entrance," he said, laughing.

If there was one thing that Jack hated more than anything else, it was being humiliated. When humiliation came in front of his family and close associates it only riled him further. In one swift movement, he pushed Diane to one side and lunged towards Macholl, grabbing the lapels of his leather jacket and thrusting him backwards. Behind, chairs scraped across the floor, as Jack's associates launched to their feet, ready to step in.

Molly froze, paralysed by fear. Harry placed himself between Molly and the commotion. She stifled a scream. The knuckles in her hand bleached white as she clutched her napkin tight.

Macholl didn't respond as he remained pinned to the wall as Jack's stale breath washed over his face.

"I've come for what's mine," Macholl demanded.

Diane's stomach twisted in knots as her body trembled. Fear flashed through her as she processed the scene.

Macholl looked past Jack's shoulder in Diane's direction.

"You owe me, 'Beanie'. You took a lot from me and left me with nothing. I spent five years banged up because of you. It could have been so different." His last few words were said in reflection more than anything else as he continued to look at Diane.

"I owe you nothing, you piece of shit. Who do you think you are, waltzing in here and mouthing off like that? Do you want this to be your last day on this planet?"

Dean Macholl offered nothing more than a smile in return. He grabbed Jack's wrists and pulled them off his jacket.

"I promise you; you will pay."

4

SILENCE ECHOED through the vehicle on the drive back to their house in Highgate. Diane knew better than to open her mouth when Jack was in this frame of mind. He had thrown his keys to the Merc in her direction and told her to drive, while he sat in the passenger seat staring out of the window, his eyes fixed off in to the distance. Ben remained silent, taking his mother's cue, choosing instead to flick through his Instagram and Snapchat feeds.

Diane occasionally glanced across checking to see if Jack's mood had changed. It hadn't. He remained tight-lipped, one arm resting on the door, the other on his lap. His hands curled in to tight fists.

The electronic gates to their house seemed to take an eternity as the black ornate railings glided open. Jack had pushed past Diane as she opened the front door. He made his way to the living room, heading straight for the drinks bar that took up the rear wall of the room.

Diane followed him in, her feet padding slowly across the marble floors.

“Are you okay? Don’t let him get to you.” She felt foolish as the words trickled from her lips. She didn’t know what else to say.

“Okay?” he seethed. His tone harsh and aggressive.

Diane froze to the spot, her arms pinned to her sides.

He threw his tumbler of whisky across the room, the glass smashing into a thousand miniature crystals as it hit the wall.

Jack had always known he would cross paths with the man at some point. What Jack hadn’t expected was that he’d have the front to turn up at a family celebration making demands.

“The piece of shit. He thinks he can just waltz in and throw his weight around demanding this and demanding that. And then he has the barefaced cheek to threaten me in front of my closest associates and family…”

“I’m… I’m sure he didn’t mean it that way, love,” she tried to reassure him.

Jack’s face contorted, trying to make sense of Diane’s words. He looked at her with an expression that questioned whether they had been at the same damn party.

“Are you for real? Are you blind or something? No one, and I mean no one has ever got away with talking to me like that. They’ve either ended up kneecapped and in a wheelchair, or buried in Epping Forest. Do you wanna go the same way?” he snarled.

Diane shook her head, and glanced towards the floor, before taking one step back. She wanted a cigarette but had left them in her handbag.

"No, I didn't think so."

Jack's rage snaked up his spine, threatening to overwhelm him. In his eyes, Diane was no better than Dean Macholl. Jack was angry at the way Dean had challenged his authority, and furious at the way Macholl had looked at Diane.

"What… What are you going to do?" she asked.

"I'll sort him," he replied as he made his way towards the front door.

She stepped in his way, placing both hands on his chest, her eyes pleading with him not to do anything. His eyes bore into her. They were cold, angry and soulless. She could feel his hot breath pounding her face.

"Don't, babes. Please don't."

He grabbed her arms and manhandled her to one side as he stepped in closer. "You don't get it, do you, you stupid bitch? No one gets away with doing that."

The words became more heated as his temper threatened to erupt once more. He tightened his grip on her arms, cutting off the circulation. His lids flickered as he narrowed his eyes.

Diane's bottom lip trembled in a mixture of fear and sadness.

All the while, Ben had waited in the hallway listening. If there was one thing he hated more than anything else, it was the way Jack treated his mum. But he was no match for Jack. At five foot six, Jack was a few inches taller than him, heavier and more violent. But that didn't stop him feeling sorry for his mum and wanting to protect her.

He stepped into the doorway and was drawn to the look of fear etched heavily in the lines on his mum's face. She glanced back and forth between her son and Jack. She felt humiliated and embarrassed in front of her own flesh and blood. Jack on the other hand turned to the side and glared at Ben.

"What do you want?" Jack spat.

Ben shuffled nervously on the spot. "Please leave her alone."

"Don't you start as well. Clear off. This is between me and your mum."

"No… No. I won't clear off. Leave my mum alone. All she has ever done is stand by your side. She hasn't batted an eyelid, or had a go at you, or even said a word about your shady deals with Mr Singh. Washing all your money through his cash and carry, and the hundred grand that you keep stashed in the spare tyres in the garage, or even the underage tarts that you shag."

Jack threw Diane to the floor, and steamed into Ben, his fists pummelling Ben's body. "I'm going to fucking kill you, and then feed you to the pigs," he screamed.

Ben cowered into a ball, his arms held across his chest in a futile attempt to protect his body. The only sound in the room was the heavy thud as each punch met its target.

"Stop! Stop!" Diane screamed as she raced over and clawed at Jack's back. "You'll kill him. He's just a boy. He's not done you any harm."

Jack threw an elbow behind him to push her off. "Get off me, woman."

Diane scrambled back to her feet and jumped on to Jack's back, throwing her arm around his neck to pull him off. She screamed and hissed.

"Take it out on me. But leave Ben out of it," she pleaded. With no signs of Jack stopping, she raked her fingers across Jack's face, the hot, searing pain forced a scream from him.

Diane backed off, fearful that her moment of red mist had lit the touchpaper. She stepped away, her hands in front of her pleading for Jack's forgiveness. Her eyes widened with terror, her body trembling in shock.

Jack rose to his feet, and slowly made his way towards Diane, who continued to retreat. She glanced beyond Jack to see the beaten and bruised body of her son curled up in a foetal position, motionless.

The veins in Jack's blood-red face threatened to rupture underneath the force of his rage. Grabbing Diane by her neck, he curled his hand into a tight fist and pulled it back. Deliberately ignoring the terror in her eyes, not caring if she lived or died, his fist raced towards her.

She closed her eyes moments before his fist crunched into her face, splitting her lip. She recoiled back, her feet trying to stabilise her as the momentum sent her body crashing backwards to the tiled floor. The dull thud echoed around the room as her head connected with the floor sending shards of pain racing through her body.

He stood over her, his fists clenched by his sides, his shoulders rounded forward. He stared at her for what seemed like minutes. Diane cried; her lips had released a torrent of blood which now seeped through her fingers as she held her face. Her legs writhed on the floor, squeals and guttural moans erupted from her throat. He pointed one finger at her crumpled body but didn't utter another word.

Jack stepped away and headed back towards the bar, grabbing a bottle of Glenmorangie but didn't bother with a glass. He looked one last time at the carnage that he'd left behind. Two battered and beaten bodies that lay twisted and broken on the floor. Jack shook his head in disgust and let out a grunt before walking out. He would spend the rest of the evening in his room at the end of the garden, planning what to do next.

5

HE HAD WALKED in this evening with three hundred and seventy-five pounds in cash in his wallet. More money than he normally took, but he felt lucky. Six hours later, he sat and stared at the three solitary pound coins on the table beside him. The sound of murmured conversations filtered into the background. Great clouds of cigarette smoke hung in the air like low-level fog, and shards of light from the ceiling poked through the haze casting a speckled glow across the tables.

His pockmarked face looked sullen and stern as he eyed the amber liquid and the golden glow of the glass-like cubes in the tumbler. He poked them with a cheap and gaudy pink plastic stirring stick to hear them jingle. Wrapping his hands around the glass, he felt the heat that burnt inside him leach into the drink. Whisky. The elixir of his life. He raised the glass and took a hefty glug, feeling the keen burn on his tongue and throat – the same burn that had made him recoil as a young boy of fourteen when his father had sneaked him into their local pub. Yet now, he longed for this feeling.

"Come on, Steve, surely you can raise my limit more?" he asked, his tone rough and gravelly.

Steve had a round face just like his brother, Terry, but being two years younger at forty-six, carried the look better as he stood there with arms folded.

"You know the rules, Pat. Before *anyone* gets a credit limit increase, they need to clear their debt first. You already owe us seven big ones. I think you've pushed your luck already, don't you?" Steve replied, leaning into Pat's ear.

Pat Skelton knew the score, but he had a master. A master that controlled every inch of Pat's mind and body. Pat had to visit him a few times a day, otherwise he feared he'd go insane. It hurt to be away for too long. He felt weak, and his body would ache and struggle to act rationally. When he finally satisfied *him*, everything seemed whole, the world was whimsical and perfect. He was all Pat needed, all Pat could ever want.

His master showed no mercy. It had only taken a few careless encounters through his betting apps while hiding in the men's toilets at work, and he'd become hooked. His master changed him into somebody that would sicken most people, but he couldn't help himself. His addiction consumed him, so much that he cared for nothing else. Everything he had once held dear fell by the wayside, his nearest and dearest, his friends, and his career. He would lie, cheat and steal for it.

Pat tried once again. "Yeah, but you know me. I'm not going anywhere in a hurry."

"It's not up to me, Pat," he replied flicking his head towards his big brother who stood overseeing a poker table.

Pat glanced in Terry's direction. It was hard to tell which of the two brothers he feared most. They were both tough, aggressive, and could switch personalities in the blink of an eye. Even though Terry had the softer face and smiled, which Steve rarely did, it was a smile that hid a violent streak that needed little provocation.

"If it wasn't for Sally, the Met would be paying their respects at your funeral. So do yourself a favour and sort your life out. You won't be getting any more credit from us. If you come back, you come back with your own cash."

Pat knew better than to argue with either of the brothers. He was treading a fine line with them. They needed him as much as he needed them. It was an uncomfortable and perverse parasitic relationship that both sides couldn't do without. He stared at the three pound coins again knowing he couldn't even afford another drink. At seven pounds a shot, the drinks were a rip-off, and the hostesses that mingled were just as rough as the cheap whisky they served.

Thinking his luck would change tonight, Pat had been on a losing streak for over a month and was desperate to claw back the thousands he'd lost. He had had weeks like this in the past where he had lost hundreds of pounds, but always turned it around.

"Get yourself home. You're done here."

Pat levelled his eyes in Steve's direction, silently pleading for one last chance, meeting nothing but indifference. There were plenty of other punters they could fleece. They tolerated Pat, he had his uses.

Dejected and lost, Pat stumbled out on to the pavement into the cool night air. The chill raced through him. He pulled out another cigarette and lit it. Pat sucked the smoke deep. He held his breath, thinking how his lungs must hate him, and smiled.

Poor dying little cells that only want me well; how can I do this to you?

"Big Issue?"

Pat turned to see a dishevelled man standing in the street. Taken by surprise, Pat stared at him with open curiosity.

"Big Issue?" Pat asked.

The man waved a copy of *The Big Issue* in Pat's face. "Yes, mate. It's my way of trying to make a few quid and get off the streets. It's only a pound. Surely you can spare a pound?"

Pat stared at him. If there was one thing he hated more than anything else, it was the beggars, scroungers and lowlifes. He had spent most of his early career dealing with such people.

Pat shook his head and turned his back on the man.

"Come on, mate. Just a quid."

"No," Pat grumbled, narrowing his eyes.

"Come on, fella, give me a break. How about a fag then?"

A pang of annoyance jolted him.

He clenched his fists. "I said no. Which part of that answer didn't you understand?"

The vagrant pulled back, his hands outstretched as he backed down. He turned to walk away and muttered "tosser" under his breath.

Pat spun around and charged at the vagrant, pushing him back against a shop window, knocking the wind from his thin frame. He glared at Pat through frightened and weak eyes. His lips twisted open to reveal crooked and stained teeth, with several gaps in between where some had fallen out.

"Listen. Stay out of my way, and if I ever see you around here again, I'll make sure you and a hospital bed become the best of friends."

The vagrant snarled and tried to wriggle free. He swung an arm in Pat's direction and spat at him. Anger coursed through his veins as Pat launched at the vagrant. The flurry of blows and knee strikes sent the dishevelled man to the floor. He coughed and spluttered as he held his face.

"Oh, man, you're killing me," he screamed as he rolled on to his side.

Pat leaned back before placing a well-aimed kick at the vagrant's stomach, followed by a few more for good measure.

The vagrant squealed and yelled as he pulled his knees to his chest.

Pat towered over the broken form and grimaced. As he looked at his hands, he felt contaminated, dirty, and soiled. He glanced around to check for witnesses. Nothing. He looked at the front of the various shops and offices. No CCTV. Good.

Steam from his hot breath floated in the still night air. Sweat beaded on his face. He bent and patted the vagrant down. The man's pocket jangled. Pat recovered a handful of loose change which on quick inspection looked to be about a tenner.

"Wanker," he grunted as he delivered one final kick before walking off.

The dull thud of his kick barely registered, the dark veil of a silent night keeping vigil.

6

DIANE STARED at her tired face in the bathroom mirror. Heavy bags circled her eyes, and her hair was straw-like and wild, but that was the least of her worries. Her bottom one had swollen to twice its size, and she looked a mess. Her head pounded, and her body ached. She could disguise the worst of it with make-up, and with an ice pack hoped the swelling would go down over the course of the next few hours. It was a practised routine that she had mastered to hide the worst of it from friends and family.

Jack hadn't returned to their bedroom last night, but that didn't surprise her. Whenever he exploded, he would take himself off to his man cave which had all the mod cons that he needed to stay away from the main house. A fully self-contained apartment at the end of the garden meant that he spent many an hour with associates discussing *business*.

After Jack stormed off, Diane had nursed Ben. She had managed to get him to his bedroom where she tended to his wounds, while she did her best to reassure him through their salty tears. There was only so much she could take, and guilt had chewed away at her all night. She had blotted out both the mental and physical pain with a bottle of wine and didn't remember passing out.

Doubts crept through her mind. Perhaps she had been stupid by provoking him further. But she couldn't stand by and see her son beaten black and blue. Or worse.

Diane headed for Ben's bedroom and quietly opened the door. She went over and stood by his bed in the semi-darkness and stared at her boy. In her eyes, he remained a boy. Her bottom lip trembled, and she winced as a bolt of pain shot through her mouth. Her eyes misted as she knelt and kissed Ben on the forehead. He lay safely tucked up under the duvet. While he was asleep, he couldn't feel any pain.

How had it come to this? Her thoughts turned to yesterday and seeing Dean for the first time in many years. Her heart had practically jumped through her chest on seeing him. He hadn't changed in her eyes. He had lost weight, but his hazel eyes still had that charm and charisma. She knew she had upset Dean. He had offered her an escape, but she had chosen Jack.

She made her way downstairs into the kitchen before flicking on the kettle to make herself some coffee. She searched through the rooms on the ground floor for any sign of Jack. Her suspicions were confirmed when she realised the house was empty. A stiff black coffee was what she needed as she ran her hands through her untidy hair, her fingers catching on the knots. She shook her head at the state of her life. She looked around her; she had everything she ever wanted. A beautiful house, luxury cars, money in the bank, and life appeared good. They took several holidays a year to Spain. She would relax in the sun, while Jack headed to Puerto Banús to discuss business with associates who couldn't step foot in Britain without being arrested.

And yet sadness accompanied her like a dark cloud wherever she went. Diane felt as if a part of her were missing, the part that would make life complete. She knew deep down that would never happen with Jack, and no amount of money or the finer things in life could give her that. But what choices did she have?

She poured boiling water into her mug and enjoyed the aroma of the coffee wafting up to meet her. She poured a second cup for Jack.

"Why are you doing this?" she muttered to herself. Despite last night, she was still being dutiful and respectful by making him coffee as she did every morning.

The crisp June morning bathed her in early warmth as she made her way down the path to the brick-built building at the end. The garden was laid to lawn with the boundary framed with ornate plants and trees, and beyond them an eight-foot wall that kept out prying eyes.

As she approached the front door, the lights were off, and she assumed that Jack was sleeping off a hangover. She knocked on the glass panel, and when there was no reply, she knocked again. Jack would always lock the door from the inside in case he had unwelcome visitors. But she tried the door handle, nevertheless, fully expecting it to be locked. To her surprise it turned, and she grimaced in confusion.

Opening the door a few inches, she called out Jack's name through the opening. Silence. The inky darkness inside offered little indication as to his location.

"Jack, are you in there?" she called, raising her voice. When there was no answer, she stepped into the hallway. To her right a doorway led to the kitchen, and to her left was the bathroom and the en suite. She called again as she moved towards the main entertaining area at the back. The curtains were drawn. In the darkness, she could see Jack leaning back in the sofa. The room had a stale stuffiness, a mixture of sweat, alcohol and a sharpness that she couldn't quite pinpoint.

She placed his coffee on the table and then went over to the window to open the curtains and window to let some fresh air in. Diane turned and froze on the spot, her body paralysed in fear and shock. At first no sounds escaped, but as the reality crept up on her, a high-pitched scream tore from her throat.

7

THE SHRILL SOUND of Karen Heath's phone jolted her awake, followed by an even larger flash of annoyance. She hated being woken up on her day off. Though she had lost count of the amount of times it had happened, she had never quite got used to it.

Last night, she'd been chilling at home, winding down as the precursor to her day off. It was just her, a bottle of Merlot, and Manky, her cat. Just the way she liked it. She lived in a small apartment in Epping, Essex. It was a two-bedroom apartment at one end of the high street, close to the Tube station on the Central Line.

Despite being so far out of town, she preferred the remoteness. Epping still carried some of the charm of an old market town, and to this day still had a thriving market that took place every Monday. The town retained elements of rurality, being surrounded by Epping Forest and working farmland. Epping had many old buildings, some of which were Grade I and II listed. Historically, it had been one of the last stops for stagecoaches when they left London en route to Norwich or Cambridge.

And that's what she loved, the history.

It was nice for her to get away from the congestion of London, and the claustrophobic atmosphere that surrounded her. She was far enough away to ensure that she never bumped into those that she arrested or came across in her line of work. Hopping on to the Tube every morning like all the other commuters gave her a sense of normality. In her job she saw the worst aspects of life, and the vilest traits that humans could display. But sitting on the Tube surrounded by those who worked in banking, insurance, retail and the service industries, helped to ground her.

Smartly dressed, she looked the part. Committed, focused, and professional. With a dry sense of humour and a formidable character, she was known for being competitive and aggressive. That was what she felt she needed to compete in a male-dominated world.

The damn phone vibrated and pinged again as it rattled across the bedside cabinet. Receiving the text message was enough for her to drag her tired body out of bed and jump in to the shower. She stood soaking her body underneath the warm spray, swearing and muttering. The first day off following a nineteen-day stretch without any breaks. She knew working herself into an early grave was wrong, and contravened every single health and safety policy, but when she signed up for the job, she waived her right to that protection.

A quick glance in the mirror to make sure she looked decent and Karen flew out the door.

Highgate was a suburb of London situated to the north, and one of the most expensive areas to live in London. Crime rates were low, and murder rates even lower. As DI Karen Heath made her way to the crime scene, curiosity tugged at her brain. She couldn't help but see the irony in the fact that the crime scene was no more than a short walk from Highgate Cemetery, a place synonymous as the final resting place to so many rich and famous from George Michael to Karl Marx.

The phrase "never a dull day" didn't exist in Karen's world. Detective Inspector Karen Heath was part of the Met's major investigation teams, more commonly referred to as MITs, that dealt with murder and attempted murder, manslaughter and infanticide offences; missing persons or abductions; and other investigations identified for specialist needs such as criminal organisations. There were twenty-four MITs that covered the whole of the Met, and she was assigned to the team that covered much of North London. It meant that her hours were long, she travelled a lot, and ducked in and out of police stations.

And the job consumed her life.

Another bugbear was Central London traffic. She was fine driving around suburbs and Home Counties, but the closer she got to town, the more frustrated she became with the congestion, the bad drivers, the taxis, the buses and well, pretty much everyone on the road. She had arranged for Detective Sergeant Jade Whiting to pick her up from a convenient Tube station.

"Morning guv," Jade had greeted her as she pulled over and flicked on her hazards.

Karen jumped in to the passenger seat and groaned with a smile. "I wish it was, Jade, but I'm shattered. I could really do without this one today. I feel so unorganised and barely had time for a shower, let alone dress properly," she said, looking at her jeans that seemed at odds with the purple blouse she had thrown on. She took a few sips of her coffee she'd grabbed from the nearby Costa while waiting for Jade. Thankfully the air was warming up, and she didn't need the warmth from the coffee, even though she cupped both hands around the vessel and hugged it close to her chest.

Jade understood and offered only a sympathetic smile. As they made their way towards Highgate, Jade updated her on the latest information to come from the crime scene. And they had plenty of time to discuss it as the Holloway Road crawled through rush hour. Karen tapped her fingers on the cup as Jade relayed the information. Jack Taylor, aged fifty-two, more commonly known as Jack 'Beanie' Taylor had been gunned down at his home. A career criminal. Identified as the head of a major criminal organisation operating in North London, with connections to Manchester, Liverpool and Spain.

Karen let out a long, deep breath as she stared at the line of snaking traffic that stretched ahead of them. Concerns rose in her mind. There could be a multitude of reasons why Taylor had been shot. A vendetta, a business deal turned sour, or a rival organisation looking to muscle in on his business.

None of Jade's actions were jerky or aggressive, which helped to settle Karen's stomach. Jade was a safe driver and had taken the advanced driver training which many officers undertook to help them with activities such as surveillance and observing suspects. She weaved in and out of the traffic, speeding up where she needed to, braking smoothly when called upon. A bottle of red wine seemed the ideal tonic last night, but it had left a dry mouth, with Karen's stomach doing somersaults when she woke this morning.

Karen flipped down the visor and slid back the cover to look at herself in the vanity mirror. She brushed through her long, dark brown hair that wrapped around her shoulders before applying eyeliner to her dark brown eyes that peaked beneath her straight cut fringe. She wasn't one for much make-up, preferring the natural look. At five foot eight she was a tall woman with an hourglass figure, which intimidated both men and women alike. A constant frown always made her look pensive as if she were assessing and analysing. To be recognised as an equal, she'd had to fight hard. But because of her tenacity, she was considered a tough and professional officer. In her early days as a uniformed officer, many of her male colleagues had teased her about her 34DD chest, and many of her female colleagues had been envious of the extra attention she attracted. Neither had been welcomed, and she now wore baggy jumpers or a blouse and jacket.

"Was there any sign of a murder weapon?" Karen asked.

"No, nothing. He was found slumped on the sofa in a building close to the main property."

"Who's over there now from the team?"

"No one as yet, guv. Brad and Steve have been called over to an armed robbery at a convenience store in Mile End. It was raided during the early hours of this morning. The manager was beaten around the head with the butt of a handgun. They left him for dead."

Karen heaved a sigh. That was all that they needed. Two big jobs at the same time, and limited resources for both.

"Has the DCI been informed?" Karen asked.

"A message has been left on his phone, but he's not answering."

Karen bristled. *Lazy pain in the arse.* The DCI seemed to have his own agenda and walked in and out of the office when it pleased him. As the DCI leading a MIT, he would be the SIO, the senior investigating officer. But Karen led the investigations then clashed with the DCI when he rebuked her for doing things without his permission.

"Any specifics on the armed robbery job?"

Jade grimaced. "Not much of a description, I'm afraid. There were three white assailants dressed in black, with black balaclavas. And check this out, there were two punters in the shop. One older guy in his late seventies and another bloke in his forties. The younger bloke shit himself and ducked under the table. The older fella got stuck in. Sadly, he was overpowered, but he slowed them down which gave us more CCTV footage. It turns out that the old boy served in the military. He's a former para."

8

THEY SWEPT through the black ornate gates, Karen showing her warrant card to the officer standing guard at the entrance. It was an impressive house in Karen's view. A horseshoe-shaped gravel driveway framed the front of the building. Green ivy crept up the walls of the double bay fronted house like a green blanket of wilderness that gave the property charm and character. Jade pulled up alongside two white scientific services vans.

"And they say crime never pays," Jade remarked getting out of the car and walking across the gravel towards the front door. "My parents had to work their socks off for a place like this!"

Jade had grown up in a similar house, and stopped for a moment to admire the splendour as her mind drifted back to her childhood. Jade was smart, polite and dedicated. She was also sophisticated young, vibrant, and determined. When she spoke, there was an air of elegance about her tone, which had earned her the nickname of 'Posh' from her colleagues. Her private schooling had made her an unlikely candidate for the police, much to her parents' disappointment. They had wanted her to join the legal profession as a solicitor or barrister.

Inner London was in marked contrast to her home in Beaconsfield, in Buckinghamshire's stockbroker belt. Her father was a financier, and her mother, an accountant, but Jade had always craved a break from suburban life, opting instead for a frenetic and crazy life in London.

"Yes, but look where it ends up," Karen replied, raising a brow. She caught sight of a Mercedes and two BMWs parked to the far side of the house.

They both signed the scene log, and acknowledged the scene guard, before taking a pack of disposable overalls and foot coverings and making their way through the house. Cream marble floors extended in all directions, and there was an exaggerated opulence about the place. Grotesque vases, prints and ornaments adorned the windowsills and fireplaces. An oversized sofa sat positioned in the middle of what Karen assumed was the lounge. Around it were tall vases, and glass tables. They walked past a TV room, a second more informal lounge, and a large kitchen kitted out in glossy white kitchen units, and black marble worktops.

Karen squinted and placed her hand above her eyes as a makeshift visor. She stepped out in to the morning sun followed by Jade. Several SOCOs dressed head to foot in white paper suits, and blue foot coverings hovered around the front door to the outbuilding at the far end of the garden. There were clear plastic evidence bags laid neatly on the floor beside one SOCO who documented all the evidence. Not wishing to contaminate the scene, Karen and Jade donned their coverings before stepping through the door. They were greeted by the brilliance of small arc lights that had been set up around the victim.

Jack Taylor lay slumped back in the cushions, his arms hung by his sides, his head tilted over the back of the sofa. Christopher Wainwright, the pathologist was putting a few things away in his bag when he saw the two officers approach. Wainwright was a tall, gangly man, with glasses, a beaky nose, and a large Adam's apple that bounced up and down in his thin neck. Of course, other than his glasses, there was little else to see as he was covered in head to foot in a white paper suit.

"Ah, Karen, good to see you."

Wainwright and Karen had worked together frequently and had developed a strong bond and mutual respect. Both shared similar traits such as their no-nonsense directness and often abrasive mannerisms.

He repeatedly asked her to refer to him as Christopher, but just to annoy him she always called him Wainwright. A joke he played along with.

"What can you tell us, Wainwright?"

"That's what I like about you, Karen, your warm, welcoming tone. I bet you're the life and soul of any party you go to."

Karen raised a shoulder. "At least I get invited to parties. You kill a conversation the minute you walk in to the room. No pun intended."

"Keep trying, Karen. One day it might work. Anyway, back to business. One victim, one gunshot wound to the head, instant death."

"Short and snappy. Just how I like it," she fired back.

Wainwright didn't respond, waiting for what no doubt would be her next question. It seemed to escape her lips in every situation like this.

"Any sign of a struggle?"

And there it is.

Wainwright smiled behind his paper mask. "There are abrasions to his face, more than likely scratch marks. But there's nothing under his fingernails. There is bruising to his knuckles, which appears to be fresh. But as you can see, there doesn't appear to be any signs of a struggle in the room. I'll know more when I get him on the table, but my first impressions suggest he was shot where he sat, and there doesn't appear to be any resistance at the time of the shooting."

"And the bullet?"

Wainwright pointed his pen towards the front door. "Forensics have it. There's an exit wound at the back of his head, which removed much of his skull. I'd say it was close range." Wainwright rubbed his chin, his eyes darting back and forth from where he stood to the corpse. "I would say about six to eight feet."

Karen moved to the side of the sofa where large blood trails had dripped down the back. There were blood splatters on the wall behind, and a congealed mess of flesh, bone and organ tissue that lay dispersed across the floor and wall.

Jade came alongside Karen and saw the evidence for herself. "He didn't stand a chance."

They discussed the possible trajectory path of the bullet. SOCOs had gouged out a small piece of plaster from the wall about twelve inches above the skirting board. Early indications suggested that the killer had stood facing Jack and had fired down towards Jack's face. Wainwright estimated a time of death between three a.m. and five a.m. as the body was in algor. He had taken body and environmental temperature readings to determine the approximate time of death.

Karen noticed that the laminate floor in front of the sofa had been dusted for footprints, as had all the door handles, glass table and whisky bottle that lay on its side.

Wainwright interrupted their discussion. "I'm off, ladies. I'll be conducting the post-mortem later, so I'll see you then." And with that, he breezed out of the room whistling to himself.

Karen stepped out in to the garden and glanced around. She frowned. "What do you notice, Jade?"

Jade looked perplexed at the cryptic question, and examined herself, thinking she'd forgotten something. She glanced back at Karen who looked around the garden. Jade followed her eyes. "Um, nice lawn, expensive rattan furniture?"

Karen tutted. "No CCTV, Jade. I noticed there was nothing at the front, and there's nothing out here. For someone of Taylor's reputation, you'd have thought this place would be protected like Fort Knox?"

"Maybe he thought he was untouchable?" Jade suggested.

Karen nodded in agreement. That was a possibility, but it made little sense to her, as she walked back towards the main house.

A FLO SAT by a woman who was hunched forward on a chair in an upstairs bedroom. Family Liaison Officers were assigned to the immediate family whenever there was a loss of life or a missing person. Despite the need to follow procedure and not discriminate, Karen felt aggrieved that a resource was being used unnecessarily. Her thinking was that, If you live by the sword, you die by the sword, and Taylor had brought this upon himself.

The FLO nodded as Karen entered the bedroom.

Karen pulled out her warrant card. "Diane Murphy?"

The woman glanced up from the mug of tea she cradled in her hands and offered the smallest of nods.

"I'm Detective Inspector Heath, and this is my colleague Detective Sergeant Whiting. We're from the Major Investigation Team. Firstly, sorry for your loss." Just saying those final few words grated. She tried to sound as sincere as possible, but noticed the dryness in her tone, and hoped the woman hadn't noticed it.

"Thank you," she whispered.

She was a short woman with a voluptuous figure. Karen put her at around five foot two inches tall, and in her late forties. With long, cascading brown locks, and piercing blue eyes, she was attractive for her age. Karen noticed that the woman's eyebrows had been plucked high above her eyes in a thin line, as if permanently fixed in a look of surprise. But behind those eyes a sadness lingered, not just from her loss, but an overwhelming shadow of loss and sadness that was clear from the lattice of red thread veins that criss-crossed her eyes.

Karen felt foolish for asking, but knew she had to. "Diane, did Mr Taylor have any recent altercations, or enemies that may have wanted to harm him?"

The question brought the slightest of smiles to Diane's face, which led her to wince as the pain from her fat lip jolted her. "You know as well as I do he probably had a string of people who wanted to have a pop at him." The question, though expected, took her by surprise. Less than a few hours ago, she had seen Jack and Dean go head-to-head. She averted her gaze from the officers, fearing her expression might give it away.

Karen pointed towards the woman's face. "How did that happen?"

Diane's face flushed, and she hastily placed her hand with a tissue over her mouth. "I had a bit too much to drink last night and fell on the steps."

Karen acknowledged the answer with a nod but wasn't convinced. "The pathologist noticed abrasions on Jack's face, and he suggested they looked like scratches. Scratches that may have resulted from a fight?" Karen let the question hang.

An empty silence tainted the atmosphere for a few moments as Karen watched the woman. Diane flicked a gaze in Karen's direction, before looking away. She looked at everything else in the bedroom other than the two officers who stood just a few feet away from her.

"You wouldn't know anything… about… it?"

As the mounting anxiety threatened to explode from her chest, Diane went on the offensive. "If you think I had anything to do with his death…"

"I'm not suggesting that, Miss Murphy. All I'm asking is whether you know how he came about those injuries to his face."

Diane shrugged and shook her head, before doing the safest thing she could do, stare at the contents of the mug.

"Well, I'll be arranging for DS Whiting here to take a full statement from you. Also, as a process of elimination, we'll need to take a buccal swab from you, and secure all the clothes that you wore yesterday."

"What's a buccal swab?" she asked.

"It's just a mouth swab so we can take a DNA profile and compare it to any evidence we come across during our investigation. It's a process of elimination. And we start with those closest to the victim."

Diane seemed to be assured by the explanation, but still looked alarmed.

Karen questioned their movements last night, and Diane explained that they had held a birthday celebration in a small Italian restaurant in Holborn, before returning to the house shortly after midnight. Karen asked for the details, before nodding in Jade's direction, who briefly stepped out of the room to organise for an officer to make their way to the restaurant to secure any CCTV footage, and to investigate the background of the guests.

"Was anyone else here last night?"

Diane stiffened, afraid to tell them about Ben. She hesitated for a few moments before muttering Ben's name.

"And who's Ben?"

"He's my son. Jack isn't his father. He was at the party last night. He's not feeling well, so I've left him asleep in his bedroom. I'll break the news to him when he wakes."

"Okay, we'll also need a swab from him. DS Whiting can do that at the same time, so you'll need to wake him."

Karen asked a few more questions before leaving. She was particularly keen to find out what time Diane had last seen Jack, as well as what time she had gone to bed. Both questions had met with vague responses that did nothing to reassure Karen.

As Karen went back to the car to retrieve her jacket, she scanned the scene once more. The lack of security still bothered her. She cast her eye back towards the house, and that's when she noticed movement in an upstairs window. From her position she could see another man, a young man. She assumed it was Ben. What she hadn't expected to see were cuts and abrasions, and the swellings around his face. She made a mental note.

9

THE ATTACK on Taylor replayed in Karen's mind. For someone with Taylor's reputation, his personal protection would have been paramount in her opinion, but that hadn't been the case when she'd looked around the house and grounds.

She ducked into a coffee shop on her way back to the station. Other than a cup of coffee this morning, she'd had nothing to eat or drink. The start of a headache was forming as her stomach rumbled. She needed time to think, away from everyone. Karen ordered herself a black Americano, and a sausage sandwich. Had Jade been with her, she would have been appalled by the saturated fat that seeped through the bottom of the bread. But as far as Karen was concerned, an indulgence every so often was something she looked forward to. Karen pulled back the top layer of bread and applied a generous amount of tomato ketchup. Air bubbles trapped in the bottle erupted as the sauce spluttered out accompanied by farting noises. She looked around smiling to see if any customers had noticed.

She felt satiated after devouring the sandwich. Ordering another cup of coffee, she flicked through the emails on her phone. The majority were circulars, internal memos, and meeting reminders. Thankfully, DCs Brad Martin and Steve 'McQueen' Nugent were back in the office having attended the convenience store this morning. Nugent had compiled a report on the system, and had emailed her with the early stages of the investigation. She rolled her eyes. If one of those two were going to take the lead, it was Nugent.

DC Brad Martin was the weak link in her team in terms of capability and competence, though she wouldn't say that to his face. A worrier and constantly fidgeting, he annoyed the hell out of her at times. He was just weird, but then again, they no doubt said that about her. She was tough, aggressive, serious at work, but fair, and that often led to friction. The fact she didn't smile much and had a dry sense of humour only made her more aloof in their eyes.

BY THE TIME Karen returned to the office, it was the middle of the afternoon. The team bobbed up from their individual workstations to see her arrive. Jade had returned from taking a statement and swabs from Diane Murphy and her son and had dropped them off with forensics.

"Okay, gather round," Karen shouted across the floor, as she positioned herself alongside the whiteboard. "Any sign of the DCI?" she asked, looking around the team. The question was met with a collective shake of their heads. *Typical*, she thought. She turned towards the board, and put a picture of Jack Taylor on the board, securing it with magnetic pins. "We've got a new case which requires our immediate attention. Jack Taylor was killed in the early hours of this morning. Often known as 'Beanie' to his associates, he was the head of an OCG."

Karen passed around printouts which included Taylor's picture, and summaries of the activities involving him. The team took a few moments to scan through the details.

She crossed her arms and rocked back and forth on her toes and heels. "As you can see, he's not your average run-of-the-mill criminal. Armed robberies, extortion and drug trafficking were key components of his business. What we need to find out is who wanted him dead?"

"That could be a big pond with lots of fish?" Jade offered.

DC Brad Martin shuffled around in his seat, head bowed, mumbling to himself.

"Brad!" Karen said firmly with a smile. "If you've got something to say, then say it, instead of muttering silent sweet nothings to yourself."

Brad's eyes widened. He hated being in the spotlight. Knowing his colleagues were staring at him, made him fidget more. Thin and gangly like Wainwright, the pathologist, Brad had a thin neck, a bulging Adam's apple, and a thin protruding chin with a matching nose. The man's nose reminded her of the shape of the Concorde's nose, thin and bent down. He winced as the muscles in his neck tightened, a problem which flared up from time to time. He'd carried the injury for ten years since falling down the stairs one night after a fight with his girlfriend.

Karen had never hung out with him other than at team dos. And even then, she never sat that close to him. He was pale, unhealthy, and pasty-looking. But she put up with him because he possessed a calculating mind which on occasion allowed him to be a brilliant problem solver.

"Yes, guv. We could talk of dozens of potential suspects, associates, enemies, rival organisations, or something even more random than that."

Brad was always the one to state the obvious.

"Thanks for that, Brad," she muttered as she turned towards the whiteboard. "We need to start looking at his final few hours, and then work back from there. Look for any falling out with anyone or another crime outfit. And while we're at it, we need to check his banking history, phone records, and emails."

"Forensics have retrieved his phones, guv. Three. And they are with the high-tech unit," Jade confirmed. But Karen knew there would be little they could recover from the phones. In her experience they often came with sophisticated encryption software that no amount of technology could crack. Any unauthorised tampering with the phones would often lead to the software detecting it and wiping the contents of the phone clean.

"Guv, Jade asked me to look at the restaurant in Holborn. I spoke to the restaurant's owners, and I also sent uniform over there to collect CCTV footage. Luckily for us they had a camera trained on the front door, and the rear kitchen door. The restaurant owners told us that everyone was well behaved at the restaurant until a former colleague of Taylor's turned up."

Having delivered his initial findings, DC Steve Nugent flicked the remote control on the TV monitor to play the CCTV footage they recovered. Steve was often known as 'McQueen'. He had earned the nickname having styled himself on his favourite actor Steve McQueen. He dressed in stylish, tight-fitting suits, with pencil-thin ties. The 'McQueen look' continued with short mousy brown hair with a side parting, and piercing blue eyes. He was suave, smart and big on appearance and styling.

Karen admired him. He was known for getting the job done, and he came with bags of confidence. He had the balance just right, and to top it off had a natural manliness to him that attracted more than his fair share of female attention. At thirty-nine years old, he was rugged and in his prime, and of all things, Karen groaned that she had to be his boss.

The CCTV footage played on the monitor. The team watched as various guests arrived. Some were familiar to them, like Diane Murphy and her son Ben, but others weren't.

"There was nothing on the front door footage suggesting an altercation, or threat of violence," Karen said. "And judging by the two burly men on the door, it was unlikely that anything would happen, unless someone had a death wish."

"No, guv," Steve agreed, as he pressed the fast forward on the remote control. "But check this out."

The footage switched to the rear kitchen doors. Nothing happened for minutes. The team grew impatient, shifting in the chairs, and sighing loudly.

"Get on with it, Steve," Karen demanded.

He paused the footage as a man with short hair and a beard, wearing a black leather jacket, approached the back door. They watched as he peered in, looking back, before stepping through the double doors. Karen made a note of the timestamp as Steve fast-forwarded the tape again to where the man reappeared through the doors and walked off. Karen made a note of that time too.

"Have you got a name for this person?" Jade asked.

Steve nodded. "The restaurant owners were reluctant to say much to begin with, but they said he was an associate of Taylor's. His name is Dean Macholl. Apparently Macholl would always be there when Taylor was meeting his other associates. But they pointed out that he hadn't been seen for a few years."

"Is he known to us?"

Steve confirmed that in response to Jade's question. "He's just been released from a Belgian prison. He did five years for robbery. Going from his case file, it was suggested that Macholl and Taylor were involved in an armed robbery of a bookies that went wrong. It resulted in a cashier being shot and fatally wounded. It was never confirmed if both were involved, but rumours on the street suggested that it was Taylor who had orchestrated the raid. After that point Macholl disappeared off the face of the earth before popping up in front of the justice system in Belgium."

"So, were there no convictions?"

Steve shook his head. "Descriptions were vague. Three white males in balaclavas. Again, rumours on the street suggested that Darren Finch, a small-time drug dealer, may have been the third accomplice. Nothing confirmed, guv."

Karen moved closer in to the monitor and looked at the frozen image of Macholl captured outside the rear doors.

"And do we know what happened inside? He was there for no more than ten minutes."

"This is where the restaurant owners clammed up. There was a heated argument between Taylor and Macholl."

"That's good enough for me. That gives us a starting point. Do we know where Macholl is?"

Steve nodded, handing her a slip of paper. The address was an apartment between Bethnal Green and Shoreditch.

"Good work, Steve. I want you to come with me. Jade and Brad, I want you to work on identifying the other faces in the video. Go back to the restaurant if you have to."

Steve was already grabbing his jacket before Karen had finished dishing out the instructions.

10

COLUMBIA ROAD WAS a mixture of modern and old. A narrow cobbled road formed the dividing line between trendy, three-storey, modern suburban living, that rubbed shoulders with older apartments, and small two-storey terraced properties. Much had changed over the past one hundred years. The ground floor of the smaller terraced properties had been converted into retail units where newsagents, knick-knack shops, and eateries stood side by side and offered an eclectic ambience to the street.

As Karen and Steve made their way along, Karen couldn't help soak up the history it offered. They walked past the Royal Oak pub, and she noticed a sign above the doorway which referred to its existence as far back as 1923. It looked like a proper East End boozer, and she wondered what tales this old establishment had been privy to.

She imagined that it had been a meeting point for many during the Second World War. A hub for the local community, a place of safety and support. In her mind, she imagined soldiers in green tunics, the Home Guard, wardens and police officers in their dark uniforms, milling about in between the raids. She wondered how many of the houses had Anderson shelters scattered in their back gardens, while other families huddled on the platforms of underground stations, protected from the barrage of bombs during the Blitz.

As they walked, the sounds of modern-day life filtered into her awareness, planes criss-crossing the sky, cars and commercial vehicles trundling along the narrow streets, and the sound of muted conversations. But back then, the sounds must have been harrowing. Air-raid sirens, and the sound of emergency vehicles as they raced from one fire to another. The images in her mind sent a shiver down her spine. London had suffered in so many ways, no more so than when Londoners heard the dull and thunderous rumble in the skies above, as hordes of German bombers clouded the skies.

And then there was the silent assassin, the flying bomb, often known as the doodlebug. She imagined the fear as each one approached. The most noticeable aspect of doodlebugs was their sound, unlike any ordinary plane. It had a strange tearing and rasping sound, more like a two-stroke motorcycle. It soon gained a sinister and disturbing quality and prompted ignoble reactions. If the motor cut out when the weapon approached, then it was likely to drop nearby, and everyone raced to the shelters; if it continued its flight, they could breathe a sigh of relief knowing it was another part of London that would fall victim.

Macholl was staying in a small and unassuming one-bedroom apartment in one of the older blocks. Karen and Steve were greeted by an eye-watering, bright yellow, communal front door, framed by two glass brick pillars on either side. At least it appeared to be safer than she expected. There was no sign of feral youths who hid their faces with black hoodies and congregated in large groups, playing drill music on their phones, and acting suspiciously.

Karen pressed the button for Macholl's apartment. The intercom crackled into life.

"Yeah?" came a man's voice.

"Is this Dean Macholl?"

"Who's asking?"

"I'm Detective Inspector Heath, and I'd like to ask you a few questions."

The front door buzzed open, and she glanced over her shoulder towards Steve. "Do you want to hang about here, just to make sure we're not interrupted or caught off guard?"

Steve shook his head and glanced around. "I don't think we're about to get jumped. Besides, I'm not going to let you see an ex-con, a violent ex-con, on your own." He humorously waved his arm, suggesting that she lead the way.

They left the hustle and bustle of the street behind them as they walked through the silent corridor. Karen scrunched her nose at the faint musty smell that mixed with disinfectant. It was a dark corridor, with cold concrete floors, and smooth walls painted in a neutral magnolia. It was better than some apartments she'd visited, where litter, and black refuse sacks sat outside each doorway, occupants too lazy to take them to the communal bins outside. She was also surprised by the absence of noise. There were no muffled sounds of screaming children behind doors, or deaf residents with TVs turned up too loud.

Macholl's place was on the ground floor. From experience many in his position often took ground-floor apartments, as it offered a means of escape, that was safer than jumping out of a first- or second-storey window.

Dean Macholl stood in the doorway of his apartment when Karen and Steve arrived. He glanced at both, his eyes narrowed with suspicion.

Karen and Steve pulled out their warrant cards, and introduce themselves, before Macholl invited them in.

It was a small apartment, and Karen noticed a bedroom to her left, which also housed a sofa, and a kitchen off to her right which appeared clean, and tastefully decorated. It had white units, with varnished woodwork surfaces. There was one doorway further on, which she assumed was the bathroom.

Macholl led them into the bedroom and sat himself on the end of the bed and offered them the sofa. It was sparsely decorated, a double wardrobe, a two-seater settee, and a bed, together with a bedside table. There were none of the personal effects that would have made it homelier, like photo frames, lamps, and prints on the wall. It was stark and bare.

"What can I do for you?" he asked with a smile.

Karen noticed that he was a tall man, at least six foot plus, with salt-and-pepper hair, and hazel eyes. When he smiled, lines creased the skin around his eyes, which left him looking weathered, but distinctive and charismatic. His grey beard added to his maturity.

Karen and Steve sunk into the two-seater sofa, and looked at each other in an awkward silence, as their shoulders rubbed, and their legs touched. The proximity to each other wasn't something they were used to.

"I'd like to ask you a few questions about an incident yesterday."

Macholl smiled in Karen's direction. It was a knowing smile as if he'd expected the visit.

"We're investigating the murder of Jack Taylor."

Macholl nodded. "So I hear."

"How did you hear?" Karen asked.

Steve took out his notebook and pen, to take his mind off the fact that the sofa was so lumpy and uneven, that it was sinking into the centre, making him lean closer towards Karen.

"Word gets around."

"We understand there was an altercation between you two at a restaurant in Holborn yesterday evening. Can you tell me what that was about?"

Macholl shrugged and smiled. He wagged his finger at them. "You're sitting here thinking I had something to do with his death. You see, your lot and I go back a long way. I know how you work. You're starting from last night and working backwards. You're checking to see what happened in the last few hours he was seen alive. And then you'll check the days and weeks before that. You'll be looking for any evidence, my movements, CCTV, his phone records, sightings of him, or any incidents connected to him. So, that's why you're sitting here now."

His assessment wasn't far off, and Karen was impressed by the man's clear and logical thinking. For someone incarcerated for five years, his thoughts were structured and rational.

"Well, I was there. As you know. We had a disagreement, but I didn't kill him. If I did, do you think I would sit here… talking to you?"

"And where did you go after leaving the restaurant?" Steve asked.

Macholl looked away, staring out of the window, the slightest of wry smiles on his face. "I came back here. As you know, because you would have done your research, I've only just returned to the UK. I popped into Mo's on the way back and came back here."

"Mo's?"

"Mohammed. He owns the off-licence down the road. He's got CCTV footage. You'll see me going in there, buying a bottle of Scotch, and coming back here." Macholl flicked his head back towards the bed, and both officers glanced past Macholl to see a bottle of Scotch sitting on the bedside table.

"So, you've just got back to the country, and you go to a private birthday party, where you kick off?" Karen asked, as she furrowed her brow.

Macholl stood up and went over to the bedside table where he retrieved a mobile phone. He flicked through the screens until he came to his messages. He passed the phone to Karen. "Someone invited me. This was waiting for me when I left the prison. The screws passed it over."

Karen read the message, before passing it to Steve, who placed it in a clear evidence bag.

"Someone other than Jack invited me, without his knowledge. I don't know who, and I don't know why. It was clear the moment I arrived that I wasn't welcome. That's why 'Beanie' kicked off."

"But you go way back. Why does he hate you?" Karen probed.

Macholl shrugged but didn't offer an answer.

"Can you think of anyone else who may have wanted him dead?"

Macholl laughed. "That list would be too long. I can't imagine him being on anyone's Christmas card list, can you? He was a dangerous man, a violent man. There would have been plenty who wanted him dead. You do know that Taylor was the supply source behind most of the drug dealers around here? He had the place sewn up."

"We'll need a mouth swab back at the station, and we'll need the clothes you were wearing yesterday."

Macholl stood, towering above the two officers, before he unbuttoned his jeans, and whipped them down in a matter of seconds, taking both officers by surprise.

Karen pushed back in the sofa. "Um, what are you doing?"

Macholl smiled, that charismatic and warm smile again. Almost teasing. "You said you wanted the clothes I was wearing. Well… I'm still wearing them." He stepped out of his jeans and pulled off his white T-shirt. "There you go. My leather jacket is hanging off the back of the door."

His approach was unorthodox but it made Steve smile, even if it surprised Karen.

Macholl walked around to his sports holdall by the side of his bed where he retrieved a fresh set of clothes.

Karen opened her handbag, and took out a pair of latex gloves, and a brown evidence bag she had folded up. She gave both to Steve and nodded for him to get on with it.

Steve shot her a look to suggest, "Why me?"

Karen fired back a stare that implied, "I'm the boss, and you can pick up his dirty crap."

Karen called through for a unit to take Steve and Macholl to the nearest station, where Macholl's formal statement would be taken, and a DNA swab would be obtained. It would also provide an opportunity to gather scrapings from under his fingernails for any evidence of gunshot residue. She requested that Brad meet Steve there to conduct the interview, while she attended the mortuary.

11

Mortuaries had a coldness about them. Not just because the temperature had to hover at a constant cool, but they had a quietness she found off-putting. People went about their work in silence, and an air of gravity and sombreness enveloped the place. Undertakers came and went. Shrouded bodies were wheeled from one place to another. And the sickly smell of death, air freshener, and disinfectant hung like an invisible cloak in the air and seeped into every fibre of the clothes you wore.

The manner of death being a gunshot wound to the face only added to the uneasy feeling roiling her stomach. Karen hadn't witnessed many bullet wounds to that part of the body. After dressing in a protective apron, foot coverings and gloves, she pushed through the double doors.

"Sorry, sorry I'm late. I've been tracking down a potential suspect." That was just the half of it. Macholl had revealed further information towards the end of their visit that provided a possible motive.

Wainwright glanced through the plastic visor that covered his face. "That's okay. I know you're busy. I was just about to start."

Jack Taylor lay on the metal trolley, the outline of his body visible beneath the white sheet that shrouded him.

"Right, shall we crack on?" Wainwright said, wiggling his latex gloved fingers. There was a hint of macabre excitement in his voice. He drew back the shroud and stood in silence for a few moments. The gunshot had hideously distorted Taylor's face.

"My word, this one is a mess."

Karen offered nothing more than a simple nod, her eyes transfixed on the remains. It never ceased to amaze her how a single gunshot could create so much damage.

Wainwright went through the standard procedure of offering visual observations of the body from head to toe. Each comment was recorded on tape and photographed by his assistant. He then moved closer to inspect the wounds around Taylor's face.

"He was shot once, with a handgun rather than a shotgun. Had it been the latter, there would have been a different shot pattern to his face as the shot dispersed. Here we have one entry, and… one exit wound," he added, lifting Taylor's head to examine extensive disruption to the back of the man's skull. "As you can see, the exit wound is larger than the point of entry. It was at close range as I thought."

"Did he try to defend himself?"

Wainwright moved down towards the man's hands, lifting each one, inspecting the palms, and the tips of the fingers, before moving to examine the back of each one. He tugged down on the inspection lamp that hung above them to offer more illumination. The hands were pale and devoid of colour as if someone had dipped the skin in a vat of bleach.

"Not that I can see, other than the bruising I observed earlier at the scene. If he had been defending himself, then his hands may have been damaged by the gunshot, or we would have been able to identify GS residue."

Karen frowned, trying to imagine the scene in her mind. If she went with what Wainwright suggested, then Taylor had his hands by his sides. Did that mean he wasn't expecting to be shot?

"However, as we saw at the scene, there are these long, thin scratch marks on either side of his face." Wainwright took a long metal probe and placed the tip on the scarring to Taylor's face. He took some moistened cotton pads and cleaned the area. "Behind the mess, we can see three scratch marks on either side of his nose that start just below the nostrils and extend across his cheeks towards his earlobes."

Karen stared at the probe. "Do you think they were done at the same time?"

"I can't be sure, Karen." Wainwright shook his head. "They are fresh, and I would say less than twenty-four hours old because there is no evidence of scabbing."

Karen thought about the possibility that the wounds had been inflicted during his altercation with Macholl. With luck, forensics would identify DNA material beneath Macholl's fingernails.

Wainwright looked up from his examination to observe Karen deep in thought, her arms wrapped protectively across her chest. "I haven't seen you over this way much. How have things been recently, since… well… you know what?"

The question startled Karen. She got on well with Wainwright, and their paths had crossed many times. He was an intelligent man, and she found herself engrossed in deep conversation with him on a level she appreciated. But it was a loaded question.

She shrugged a shoulder, unsure how to respond. They had always been frank and open with each other, but one area had been a sticking point in recent times.

Accepting Karen's awkwardness, he attempted to appease the situation. "Listen, I know it can't be easy. It's me, Karen. I think I know you well by now. It's been a difficult journey for you, but I want you to understand that my door is always open, and the kettle is always warm."

She offered a smile in return. "Only if you've got chocolate digestive biscuits," she added, injecting humour to lighten the situation.

Wainwright's head tipped back, as he roared with laughter. "A woman after my own heart. I'm sure I can stretch to that… because it's you." Wainwright pushed no further. He had said what he needed to and left an open-ended invite.

Wainwright moved back to business. "So yes, your cause of death is a gunshot wound to the head. But I will also continue with my examination and open the big fella up and see what else we have. At the scene, I noticed that he had a slight yellowing to his skin in places. That could indicate many things, but my instinct tells me that based on his lifestyle, it could be early liver disease from excessive alcohol consumption."

Karen sighed. "Thanks, Wainwright. I'll await your full report. Right now, I need to call it a day. I had an early start, and frankly, I'm shagged."

Wainwright raised a brow in response to Karen's bluntness and winked in return.

12

Karen's stomach growled as the aroma of food filled her kitchen. The microwave chimed three times as it finished cooking a meal. She opened the door and was hit with a wall of heat and steam as her Italian pasta bubbled and spat in its plastic container. She gripped the edges and whipped the dish out, the searing heat from the plastic scorching her fingertips.

"Hot, hot!" she fumed, waving her hands in the air.

She'd followed the instructions and waited a further minute. While waiting, she grabbed a large wine glass and helped herself to some red wine. She'd talked herself out of labelling the habit alcoholism, but Tesco's over the road did a healthy trade in wine from her, and half a bottle miraculously disappeared most nights she stayed in. She could blame stress, boredom, or loneliness. Any of them, or all three. But she didn't care. She loved how it blotted out the worst of her thoughts at the end of the night.

Karen dropped into her sofa and let the cushions hem her in. With her plate on her lap, and vino by her side, she let out a sigh of relaxation. She felt too tired to eat, but knew she needed to. Mental exhaustion could roll into physical exhaustion, and she often found herself having a few pieces of toast before collapsing on the sofa and waking up in the middle of the night, not remembering when she'd dozed off.

She flipped through the channels, but nothing seemed to seize her attention. She grabbed her other remote control and changed to Netflix. There were a few series that she was following, some were crime dramas, others were one-off thrillers, and some were just plain light entertainment that required little effort on her part.

She forked pasta, taking in large mouthfuls. It wasn't until she ate that she realised how hungry she was. Other than copious amounts of coffee during the day, she had survived on nothing more than a sausage sandwich from the café this morning.

Manky, her cat, padded in and rubbed his body against her legs. He had been lying on her bed, his favourite place, until the smell of food piqued his curiosity. He purred his approval as Karen rubbed the side of her foot against his thick coat. She'd had Manky for three years and had only bought him once she'd found a place that allowed her to keep pets. He was a Great British short-haired breed, with the densest of coats, that felt plush. He was easy-going and slept most of the day, which made life easier. He was kind, loyal, loved a cuddle, didn't answer back, and gave her little to worry about.

She blew him a kiss as his bright copper eyes stared at her.

"If you think you're getting any of this, think again, boyo. Your dinner is in the kitchen. If you're lucky, you might get a treat later."

Manky remained expressionless as he looked her up and down. She had named him Manky when she had visited the litter not long after they were born. There was something about him that drew her in. His ears were curled forward much in the same way as rugby players who have cauliflower ears. And instead of a high-pitched squeal and cry that his brothers and sisters offered as they clamoured for her attention, Manky could only muster a croak. She thought he looked manky and the runt of the litter, but his description soon became his name.

After finishing her meal, Karen placed her plate to one side and took a few healthy glugs of her wine and enjoyed the wave of euphoria that flooded through her. She closed her eyes, and let the tension fall from her shoulders, savouring the moment.

The moment of escape soon passed as she reached for her laptop and logged in. There was something about Dean Macholl that bothered her. He had an edginess to him, but equally had the face of a charmer. He had come across as placid and intelligent when she'd questioned him at his apartment. She searched through the databases until she identified his files. What she read appeared to contradict the initial impression she'd formed of him. Reading through the details of the botched raid on the bookies, and the subsequent fatal injuries sustained by the cashier, didn't fit with the man she'd met. At some point in his life, Dean Macholl had been a violent armed robber.

Perhaps he's done his time and is turning over a new chapter in his life?

"And pigs can fly," she muttered to herself. Who was she kidding?

While online, she checked on the progress of the other case that her team was dealing with. Steve and Brad had updated the files to confirm that CCTV footage captured the raid, but couldn't identify any suspects from the footage. Forensics had completed their sweep of the premises. They had found dozens of fingerprints on the glass door, handles, work surfaces and TV screens. While that was good, Karen knew it was like searching for the proverbial needle in a haystack. She had no doubt that most of the prints belonged to customers.

Her mind swirled as she dropped the laptop on the couch beside her, and tilted her head back for a moment. It was the new case that was spinning her mind, or the red wine.

She glanced at Manky, who was asleep and blissfully unaware of the turmoil that raced through her mind. Being alone afforded her the peace and tranquillity she needed. And being in a small market town offered her the anonymity she wanted. But at that precise moment she would have loved a few hours in the company of a man. Perhaps not even a few hours if she thought about it. In fact, she knew she'd be an awful girlfriend, and a nightmare to live with. But with the wine flowing, her body ached for some raw, passionate sex. The type where she could throw caution to the wind and enjoy the fantasies she kept hidden. The thought of being in a physical relationship, or any relationship for that matter with the same person for years frightened her.

She hadn't been like other officers going through the ranks. As a police constable, she'd seen many of her colleagues enter casual relationships with each other. When she had rebuffed the unwanted male attention, rumours had spread about her being a lesbian… just because she didn't conform.

Her relationship with the DCI had been anything but harmonious. The rumours about her sexuality continued to the day. He had tried a clumsy and drunken pass at her during a Christmas party. He hadn't taken kindly to being brushed off, to which he'd replied "you will regret this." The air had crackled with tension in the days that followed, and they had never seen eye to eye since. He was a dick-head in her opinion. An officer that should have retired long ago. Karen suspected that he was the source of many rumours about her. The DCI carried a lot of clout, he was old school, and well respected. Karen, on the other hand, was a pariah, not liked by many. She played by the rules and wouldn't think twice about grassing on officers who bent or broke the rules.

She had seen more than her fair share of blackmail and corruption. In her eyes, such officers blackened the name of the Met and the fantastic job they did. The rank and file were lambasted by the press, criticised in Parliament and not trusted by the public.

"Why… why… why am I so screwed up…?" she mumbled as her body succumbed to sleep.

13

THE SMELL of the wine from last night added to the nausea that ebbed and flowed through her. The thirst stayed after each slow drink of water, but her head felt fit to crack open.

It was the same every day. It always felt like a great idea when she poured herself a glass most evenings, choosing to ignore how crap she would feel the next morning. But in the cold light of day, she regretted every mouthful as she sipped on her bottle of water.

She stepped through the gates of the car park at the back of the station and made her way to the rear entrance. Karen had seen Steve ride in before her. She smiled to herself. There was nothing conventional about Steve's approach. Most mornings, he rode in on his bike, a 1966 Triumph TR6 Trophy. Why had he picked that model? Because his idol had ridden one. Steve had gone to great lengths to explain why he had chosen it. Karen had forgotten his reasons the moment the words left his lips. To her it was just a bike, a great-looking bike, but for Steve it was a part of history.

"Guv," Steve said as they joined each other at the door. He ran his fingers through his hair to bring it back into some shape, having removed his helmet.

Even with his hair ruffled, he still looked suave and rugged. If she'd ridden a bike to work, she would have looked like a washed-out cat.

"Morning, Steve. How's you this morning?"

"I'm good. How about you? Did you have a good evening?"

"The usual. Wine, food, and TV. We live exciting lives don't we?"

"Some say we do. No two days are the same. We deal with shit, we shovel the shit, and we hate that shit."

"So, you love your job then? That's a ten out of ten on the job satisfaction scale, right?" She laughed.

Steve didn't answer as he laughed at his own assessment.

"Did you have a good evening?" she asked.

"Nothing amazing. Like yourself. Just a quiet one."

"No hot dates?" she teased.

Steve narrowed his eyes pretending to contemplate. "Me or you?"

Karen's face flushed red in embarrassment.

He held the door open for her, and she stepped through, waving at the duty sergeant as they made their way to the office.

"Don't tell me, you watched *The Great Escape*… yet again! What are you up to now fifty, sixty times?"

Steve smiled, not rising to the bait. "It's still a classic, guv. I'll have to get you to watch it at some point. Then you'll be a convert."

Karen shook her head and smiled. "No chance. Don't get me wrong. He's a great actor, but I've been through enough Christmases and still not been tempted."

"There's always a first time, guv," he said with a wink.

She enjoyed being around Steve in much the same way as the others. She had a good team behind her. They trusted her even though she could be forceful and direct in her approach. They worked well together, and other than Brad, it was a strong team.

The station was a hub of activity as it was every day. Officers filtered in and out of rooms, prisoners were being processed in custody, and the wheels of justice turned slowly.

Whichever station she walked into, she still got the odd look from officers. And this station was no different. They would glance at her as she walked past. A sneaky look from the corner of their eye. It was something she had never got used to, nor would she. It was the Chinese whispers, and the look of disgust that seemed to be etched in their eyes whenever she was around. It was a blot on her career that had led to all of this.

She had only been back at work eight months after suspension, riding in the second of two unmarked police cars. The convoy had been ambushed by assailants with baseball bats and sawn-off shotguns. The vicious attack had left two police officers from the leading car dead, and led to the subsequent kidnap and death of Anne Woodland. Anne had witnessed an attack on a high-end wine bar that resulted in one member of staff being shot and killed, and the unmasking of the three suspects as they made their getaway. She later identified them, and the case went to court. Anne had been assigned protection and was being transported to court at the time of the attack. The case fell apart after Anne went missing and the woman was later found bound and shot in the head on farmland near Chelmsford.

Shock and anger rocketed through the station after the incident. Losing police officers in the line of duty was a thankful rarity, and a huge blow to the Met. The incident had cast an unwelcome spotlight on the force, and every officer that served within it. Everyone in the aftermath was vociferous in their condemnation of Karen and her team. She had been the SIO on the case and had withstood searching questions from the Met's DPS, the IPCC, the Home Secretary and the Commissioner.

Karen had barely survived the witch-hunt, and the need for a scapegoat. There had been no threat made to Anne Woodland after she had identified the men. But it later transpired that all three men had connections to the Connells, a major London crime family. Whether it was a sanctioned hit by the Connells was unclear, but their name had remained on the radar since.

In hindsight, greater security measures should have been taken. And they would have been if they had discovered earlier the connection with the Connells. Karen had carried the can and just avoided being dismissed from the force for potential negligence. Instead, she'd accepted a suspension and demotion from DCI.

Uncovering those involved in the attack remained unfinished business in her mind. It was something that plagued her and would haunt her every day if she allowed it. Feeling inept at the job she loved left her checking and double-checking every piece of evidence gathered on the cases she oversaw. She would scrutinise suspects, take a hands-on approach to the investigations, and never leave her team to do all the legwork. She couldn't afford to face another mistake again.

Never, ever again.

Karen knew senior officers, and the Commissioner were watching her every move and waiting for the opportunity to justify their lack of faith in her. The way Skelton blew hot and cold provided one more reason to hate the DCI. He was often absent without explanation and flitted between moments of support for her and barbs of condemnation. If there was one person she needed support from, it was him. Feeling alone and isolated, she battled hard to hold on to her place on the force, and her sanity. She wondered if the rumours about her would ever go away. She questioned if the force would trust her again, and she contemplated whether she could fight like this every day, every week and every month until she retired.

Every single day since the attack, the incident replayed in her mind. The drive from Camden, the van slowing in front of them as they made their way along Agar Grove, the 1960s four-storey council flats that she had stared at as they drove past, and then pandemonium. Both unmarked vehicles were hit from the side as two cars pulled out from parking bays. Everything after that point seemed to happen in slow motion even though it lasted just a few seconds.

The violence, threats and the confusion played out vividly through her thoughts. Her mind had spun, her attention being pulled in every direction. Men screaming, firearms being waved around, and car windows being smashed with baseball bats. She'd never forget the chilling screams of terrified members of the public who ducked down behind parked vehicles for cover, and the shouts and panic from inside the transport vehicle as Anne was hauled out of the lead car and bundled away. And then the gunshots rang out and echoed around the surrounding buildings. She recalled the silence that followed, as if someone had muted the sound. Shocked, with hearts pounding, and adrenaline surging through their veins, the remaining officers raced to their fallen colleagues. Her last memory was the screech of tyres shattering the silence as the attackers raced away.

The wine helped to push those memories back into the dark box that nestled deep inside her mind, and the solitude of her apartment stopped her from feeling claustrophobic and suffocated.

But one thought kept rushing back, unwelcome and unbidden. She couldn't control it. How did the attackers find out that the chief witness in a major trial was being transported across town? The details of the journey had been kept secret with just the officers in the cars and their superiors being informed. As far as Karen was aware, they hadn't been followed, and none of the officers had let slip about the major operation. For the last few years, several intelligence-led operations against a major OCG in London had been thwarted, the intended targets disappearing moments before the police arrived.

Every opportunity to expose and bring down the Connells had resulted in failure which could only lead to one conclusion.

They had a mole.

Someone on the inside had betrayed them.

14

THE TEAM GATHERED EARLY as the smell of instant coffee and bacon sandwiches wafted around the room. Being a major investigations team, more than a dozen other officers and support staff were available and present for each briefing. The additional members of the team conducted much of the legwork, reviewing of witness statements, data inputting and cross-referencing on the HOLMES2 system. The data inputters and support staff played a vital role in every major investigation. They input the details of every phone conversation, interview, evidence record and all lines of enquiry undertaken. It was a massive undertaking. An exhibits officer was assigned to the investigation to log every item seized or recovered such as mobile phones, keys, items of clothing, and weapons.

Karen would always relay the information to those who worked closest to her, and they would work with the remaining members of the team. It wasn't unheard of for the team to swell to over fifty officers on major cases. And if Karen didn't make inroads, then the likelihood would be that the team would grow to that size.

There was the usual rumble of background noise, small pockets of conversation that filtered around the room. Some related to the case, others were personal conversations between colleagues who aired their grievances, annoyances and heartache in life to each other.

Karen cleared her throat as she scanned the briefing room. "When you're all finished discussing how insignificant your lives are, we can begin. And the next person who whispers under their breath will have to fork out for a tray of pastries for everyone here."

There was a ripple of laughter amongst those gathered.

"Right. Hopefully you've had time to get up to speed with the case. We've got Jack Taylor dead in the mortuary. I have confirmed the cause of death to be a gunshot wound to the head. There were other health-related issues, which are in the report, but played no part in his death."

"Guv, is Macholl still a lead suspect?" A voice came from the back of the crowd.

"He's not been ruled out, put it that way. He's the last person that we know of who had an altercation with Taylor. All those who attended his birthday bash witnessed it. So, he remains a suspect.

"We've formally interviewed him. Early indications suggest that he had a plausible motive. He believes he was stitched up by Taylor."

"Any news from ballistics?" Jade asked.

Karen confirmed that Steve would update the team on that point. "I need you to chase forensics and see if they were able to retrieve anything from Macholl's clothing."

She stared at the incident board which now included pictures of the crime scene, and detailed images of the post-mortem. She lingered on the images of Taylor's head.

Steve confirmed that ballistics was still doing an analysis on the bullet recovered from the wall. All they could confirm for the moment was identifying the murder weapon as a small handgun.

A member of the forensic team present at the briefing stood up and offered further details on the processes they would use. Karen thought it would benefit members of the team who had not been involved in firearms incidents before.

Angela from forensics explained that when a firearm was discharged, it released a cloud of gases and fine particles composed of gunshot residues. The mixture would often contain both organic and inorganic particulates. The organic matter comprised unburnt and partially combusted propellant and inorganic matter produced by hot gases acting on the bullet.

The team remained silent as heads turned towards Angela, listening with curiosity.

Angela added that these fine particles would settle on any nearby surfaces and were easily carried away from the scene.

"Thank you," Karen said. "So, I'm hoping we identify some of that residue from Macholl's clothing, and if so, that would place him at the scene."

"What else do you need us to do, guv?" Brad asked.

"I need you to do the usual. Phone records, bank records, and CCTV footage. In fact, CCTV footage is our best chance. We've got Macholl at the restaurant. We know Taylor left the restaurant after midnight. And he was probably home around one a.m. Diane didn't discover him until nearer eight a.m. So, we need to pin down Macholl's movements between those hours."

"I'm checking the CCTV footage from the off-licence," Steve confirmed.

Karen nodded her approval. "And while you're doing that, organise a search for any other CCTV footage from his street. Check the pub, his apartment block, and the other shops in the street."

"That could be dozens of hours of footage, guv, if not hundreds, if we find enough feeds," Steve suggested.

"Well, you better get started then."

Steve didn't groan or throw his pen down in annoyance or show any other signs of dissatisfaction. He nodded, and took it on the chin like the consummate professional he was.

"I need you all to check and double-check the list of guests. Especially his associates. Track them down and find out as much as you can. I doubt you'll get much from them. Honour amongst thieves and all that bollocks. But lean on them nevertheless. And if they give you grief, then suggest that they could be charged for withholding information."

Jade wafted a sheet of paper above her head to get Karen's attention.

Karen nodded in her direction.

"It's not the first time that we've had something like this, guv. I checked the records for a similar MO and a couple of years ago we had another unsolved case in Whitechapel. It was a known drug dealer, shot through the head. He had links to the Connells. The investigating team hit a brick wall, but their informants implied that the victim had ripped off the Connells. Of course, nothing could be confirmed, and they couldn't find any links back to the Connells. Even some CCTV footage disappeared."

Just hearing the name of the Connells sent a shot of adrenaline through her system. Karen stiffened. "Okay, Jade. It might be unrelated, but because it's the Connells, can you look into that?"

Jade nodded her agreement.

"Anything else while we're all together?" Karen scanned those present. Some looked bored, others stared at their notepads, and the rest just glared at her solemn-faced. "Don't look too excited!" she quipped.

Brad broke the silence. "Oh guv, the manager from the convenience store is awake and due for release. We've had armed officers stationed with him at the hospital. He hasn't been able to give us much, other than the assailants were three men, IC1, dressed in black with balaclavas and gloves. He said all of them were heavyset. I'm afraid that's it at the moment. He sounds pretty dazed."

"Okay, Brad. Keep me updated. If anyone needs me, Jade and I will be paying Diane Murphy another visit. Let's get to work."

Karen stood outside the closed door of DCI Pat Skelton's office, a sliver of annoyance crawling up her spine. He always kept his door shut, choosing to distance himself from those around him. As she had learnt this morning, the DCI had called in yesterday saying he was unwell and feeling sick. Karen had a different view on it. Every time she had been near him, the distinct and unpleasant odour of cigarettes and stale booze had assaulted her nostrils. His gravelly voice, bloodshot eyes and low-hanging jowls, made him look old and weathered. And at fifty-eight years old, he was certainly both of those to look at. He had done his time in the force but had remained on for reasons Karen never understood.

As she knocked at the door, Skelton shouted, "In!"

The familiar aroma of a brewery greeted her as she entered his office. He glared at her from the other side of the desk. There was no formal greeting, let alone a smile. Not even a slight baring of teeth. Skelton was dressed in a dark grey suit, with a white open-necked shirt, and a tie loosely hung around his neck. Over the years, his hair had begun to inch back ever so slightly, which now left him with a large forehead.

Karen stared at the dark heavy circles around his eyes. His eyes gave nothing away as he crossed his arms and leaned back in his chair.

"Karen, I wondered where you were. I understand we've got a live one? Is there any reason I wasn't called yesterday to oversee the start of the investigation? I am the SIO."

"Sir, I looked yesterday, but no one knew where you were. They only brought it to my attention this morning that you had called in sick yesterday. And had I known, I wouldn't have disturbed you anyway." Karen tried to sound as sincere as possible, knowing full well that it pissed him off. She had taken the limelight while he was away, and he didn't like that.

"It doesn't matter whether or not I'm off, you should have kept me in the loop." The clipped words flew from his tight lips as he threw his pen across the desk. Skelton was in a bad mood. Only moments before Karen had entered, he had received a call from the Connell brothers chasing payment against his tab. He had tried to bluff his way through the conversation, desperate to buy himself some time. Payday was just three days away. If he could keep them at bay until then, he could throw a few hundred pounds their way in the hope it would buy him a slight reprieve.

"Yes, sir," Karen replied, trying to move the conversation along. She updated the DCI with the salient points, leaving out the things she felt he didn't need to know. She touched on the circumstances around Taylor's death, his altercation with Macholl, and the lines of investigation she had followed.

Karen also briefed him about the armed robbery at the convenience store and what was now a case of attempted murder. She talked about it being a similar MO to a previous unsolved case, and how that victim was linked to the Connells.

Skelton held a firm stare, his mind bouncing from one possibility to another as his fingers tapped away on the desk. "I'd be surprised if this case, or the other unsolved case you're referring to had anything to do with the Connells. I've heard nothing that might suggest they were involved recently in armed robberies. I think it's possibly misguided on your part. I would suggest that you pay more attention to Taylor's murder, than the bookies."

"Well, that's my intention anyway, sir. Taylor was a big name in the criminal underworld. He carried a lot of clout, and my concern is that this could be even bigger than just the murder of Jack Taylor."

Skelton scratched his nose. "Bigger? What's bigger than Jack Taylor on our patch?" he questioned.

"Well, sir, Taylor headed up a large organisation. And we know that he was involved in the supply of drugs. We've not been able to find anything that suggests that he was importing the drugs. So, that means it's highly likely that there had to be a bigger outfit higher up the chain bringing in the stuff. Who do we know on our patch who's bigger than Taylor?"

Skelton raised a questioning brow.

"The Connells."

Skelton shook his head. "I doubt it. I'll support you in whatever you do, but I'd suggest looking lower down the fruit tree. The Connells wouldn't waste their time with the likes of Taylor. Start on the streets. My guess is that Taylor pissed off a dealer and paid the price."

"You think?"

Skelton nodded empathically. "Don't waste our time and resources on the Connells. You'll end up going around in circles. If they were involved, and I say *if*, they wouldn't be so stupid as to have anything that ties back to them. Okay?"

"Understood, sir," Karen replied as she stood to leave.

"Shut the door on your way out."

Once the door had closed, Skelton cradled his head in his hands and blew out his cheeks. He stared at the closed door for the next few minutes as his mind raced and his nerves jangled. He grabbed his phone from his jacket and punched the redial button.

15

Molly stared at her mother with a mixture of despair and anger. Her mum rarely seemed to move from the sofa. Empty mugs, beer and wine bottles, and silver foil wraps lay discarded around her. Molly recalled her mum being a happy soul many years ago. They never had much money, but they managed to get by. Their clothes were second-hand from the charity shop, food came via donations from the food bank, and her mum occasionally smiled when she was off her face. For as long as she could remember, it had been just her and her mum. She had never known her dad, and her mum had been reluctant to tell her much about him. Being a single parent was nothing new on their estate. At least half the families only had one parent.

It was a run-down estate with social and economic problems. A diverse population of residents only added to the lack of cohesion. Black, Chinese, Bengali, Eastern European, and even the odd scattering of Syrian refugees led to fragmentation rather than integration.

But Molly and her mum got by and had each other. That all changed when her mum met Finch. He ran the A10 gang and intimidated the estate. Finch had come up with the name because they lived close to the A10, and most gangs labelled themselves based on the area they lived in or their postcode. Molly thought the whole gang name thing was pathetic and immature just like Finch. But Finch had seen her mum as a soft touch, and had charmed her with cash, presents and, primarily, attention. Her mum hadn't had sex in years, and now Molly had to put up with her mum moaning and groaning in the next bedroom, or worse, on the couch because that's where Finch had decided to have her regardless of whether or not they were alone. He had wormed his way into their family.

And that had been her mum's downfall.

Finch had introduced a lonely single mother to drugs. At first, he told her that it was just for fun. But the more she took, the more she relied on it, and the greater the control he had. It got to the point where she would do anything for him. And that turned into being a mule. He would send her on small errands with packets of drugs stuffed down the front of her knickers. In return he kept her hooked and compliant.

Molly hated to see her mum so helpless. Since Finch appeared on the scene, the woman was nothing more than skin and bones, with sunken eyes, cracked lips, and dishevelled hair. Molly couldn't remember the last time her mum had taken a shower. *Perhaps four or five days ago?*

If Molly didn't scrape enough coins together to go down to the launderette, none of their clothes got washed. Each week, she gathered essentials that needed washing. She would start with socks, tights and underwear, and if there was enough space, she would do the rest.

Under the thumb of drugs and abuse, her mum had become a feeble person, scared of her own shadow. But that hadn't always been the case. Finch was to blame. He had manipulated and terrorised her to a point where most days she was a zombie. Molly recalled a time when Finch had grabbed her mum by the throat and pinned her to the wall. His eyes bulged, his breath was hard and furious, and spittle rained down on her mum's face as Finch screamed at her. Her mum had done nothing wrong; it had been part of the conditioning process. He had threatened her mum saying he would cut off her hands if she grassed on him.

Molly had stood frozen to the spot. She had wanted to step in and pull him away, but that would have infuriated him further. And she was no match for him. She knew about the cash, drugs and guns he hid in her mum's bedroom. But she would never dare say anything.

Whenever Molly was at home, she carried a deep ball of anxiety in the pit of her stomach. She always worried during Finch's visits. Recently, he had paid her more attention, and she hated the way he leered at her, his eyes undressing her. A desperation in his words when he reminded her, "You'll be ready for me soon."

The familiar double toot of a car horn jolted her from her thoughts. She went towards the front of the apartment and peered out through the window to see Harry waving at her through the car window of his red Saab 93. Just the sight of his face lifted her mood. She had been with Harry for thirteen months, and so far, they'd been the happiest of her short life. He had a way of chasing the bad things away, the misery, anxiety and sadness. He'd promised her that when the time was right, he'd take her away from the crappy Copthorne council estate, and the crime.

Harry knew her deepest, darkest secrets. She'd confided in him about her home life, her mum and Finch. He'd been incensed, threatening to run Finch over, but Molly had begged him not to make her situation worse.

Molly grabbed her bag and made for the front door, not bothering to close it quietly. She doubted her mum would stir as the door slammed in its frame. Her shoulders dropped, and Molly let out a sigh as she stood in the walkway that ran across the front of all the apartments. Waves of relief flowed over her every time she left the apartment.

She bounced down the steps, a sense of excitement growing. The prospect of seeing Harry and feeling his warm protective arms around her filled her with joy.

As she reached the last step and turned the corner, she collided with the bulky frame of a man. Bouncing off his chest left her stunned and disorientated. She looked up ready to apologise for walking into him, when her eyes widened in fear.

"Where are you going in such a hurry?" Finch asked, as he fanned his arms out by his sides to block her path.

Lost for words, Molly tried to sidestep him, fear driving her on to put as much distance between herself and Finch.

"I'm meeting Harry downstairs."

Finch narrowed the gap between them. He took one step forward as Molly took one step back. She moved to her left, and then to her right, Finch matched her move for move. She backed away from him until her back hit a wall.

Molly glanced around, desperate to move away, but Finch caged her in.

She could feel his warm, stale breath stroking her face. Molly scrunched her nose as her heart pounded in her chest, every muscle in her body willing her to run.

"You don't want Harry. He's just a boy. He probably hasn't started shaving. You need a real man," he insisted as he pressed his body against hers.

Molly closed her eyes and turned her head away, desperate to blot out the image of Finch's disgusting face.

"I know about the drugs and money!" she screamed. "I know you've stolen from Jack because I heard you tell Mum. I won't say anything. Please just leave me alone."

Finch grabbed her face, his thumb and fingers pressing into her cheeks as he turned her face towards him. "Do you think that bothers me? He's dead. Lying somewhere in a fridge with a bullet in his head. He's gone and I'm top dog around here now. Your mum can have all the gear she wants now. Bags of the stuff… for free."

Molly pleaded and tried to squirm away from him.

He bent down and inhaled as he smelt her hair. His body responded, his cock throbbing in his jeans. He pressed his groin into her. With his other hand, he groped her small firm breasts. His breathing quickened, but for different reasons than Molly. Finch stepped back and looked her up and down, desperate to ruin her for any other man. "They're getting a right decent size, a proper handful," he growled as he fixed his stare on her chest.

Finch pulled a wad of notes out of his pocket and thumbed through them.

Molly had seen him do this before in front of her mum. Her mum's eyes would light up, hoping Finch would spare her a few notes. Cruelly, he would stuff the cash back in his pocket and laugh in her face. Molly hated seeing the light fade from her mum's face. She wondered if Finch could stoop any lower… probably.

Here he was, teasing her in much the same way.

Finch separated a few tenners from the rest and stepped in towards Molly. She pressed herself further into the wall, wishing it would swallow her whole.

He grabbed Molly by the waistband of her jeans and pulled her into him. She gasped, her eyes fixed in a terrified stare. He thrust the tenners down the front of her jeans.

"You better get used to this; your pussy will earn a lot more than that soon. I reckon we could get thirty quid a pop. Don't worry about it. The boys in the crew will break you in. Then the punters can have sloppy seconds."

Finch roared with laughter.

The bile rose in Molly's throat, and her stomach lurched before she spun around and vomited. She grabbed the stair rail as her knees buckled and sweat beaded her forehead.

"I'll enjoy you soon. Don't worry, all kids your age find it hard to begin with. I'll be gentle… like fuck I will," he shouted as he walked past her towards the apartment. His guttural laugh echoed around the walkway.

Molly stood frozen to the spot. She willed her legs to move as she wiped away the puke that dripped from her chin. Her body trembled, as her mind experienced a storm of confusion and fear. Tears moistened her eyes, but she wiped them away with the back of her hands. She was desperate for

Harry not to see her in this state. Molly tipped a few bits of spearmint chewing gum into her mouth and straightened her clothes.

She ran down the remaining flight of stairs and towards Harry's car. Molly flung the door open and jumped in. She greeted him with a smile and a quick peck on the cheek. "Drive, please drive. Get me away from this shithole!"

"You okay? You look well red in the face?" he asked, a look of concern etched in his features.

Molly nodded, as she glanced out of the window on her side, scared to look at Harry in case she broke down. "Yeah, just drive, babes."

"Anything for my princess." He smiled as he turned the car around and sped off through the estate.

16

As Karen and Jade pulled into the curved driveway, a lone police officer stood at the entrance, keeping unwanted visitors at a safe distance, including the press. SOCO had done their investigations and left Diane to herself. A FLO kept her company, being the conduit between the investigating team and Diane.

"Do you think you'll get more from her, guv?"

"That's the plan. It might come across as insensitive considering her loss, but we need to keep the pressure on. It's not your ordinary family, living in suburbia, with two point four kids. There'll be plenty she'll know… information we need."

Diane answered the door after Karen had rung the bell twice. She offered nothing more than a nod as she stepped to one side to let the officers in. Diane led them to the lounge and deposited herself in an armchair, Karen and Jade trailing after her. Jade stood, casually walking around the room, inspecting prints on the walls and photos above the fireplace.

Diane kept her eyes on Karen, unaware of Jade's movements in her peripheral vision. The older woman looked tired and stressed. She was dressed in a pair of tight black jeans and designer T-shirt. A lack of make-up, or slap, as Karen often called it, made Diane look older. With her pale and flat skin, the age lines became more prominent. And despite the blandness of her appearance, those excessively high eyebrows still stood out. Karen felt her stare drifting from Diane's eyes to the woman's eyebrows.

"Any reason you're back so soon?" Diane asked, her voice monotone and drawn out. "I have a funeral to plan."

"We won't take too long, but I suspect this will be one of many visits we will pay you, considering Jack's background."

Diane stiffened, sternness tightening her features. "We're the victims here. Jack's been murdered. Is this how you treat all victims' families?"

"There are a lot more motives for Jack's murder than the average member of the public. And because of that, it means we have to dig deeper. We'd like to ask you a few questions about the night he was murdered."

Diane shrugged. "As long as it doesn't take too much time. I have lots to do."

"We've spoken to Dean Macholl. He showed us the message on the mobile phone given to him as he left prison. Do you have any idea who might have sent him that message?"

"I haven't got a clue."

Karen nodded. "How many people knew about the birthday party, other than those who attended?"

After a few seconds, the penny dropped, and Diane's face took on an inquisitive look as her brow furrowed. "As far as I know, no one. Only the restaurant staff and the guests knew about it. We wanted to keep it a surprise. So, the fewer that knew, the better. I can't speak for the others, but I didn't say anything."

"We are working through the list of attendees. But was there anyone around the table who had a vested interest in setting up a confrontation so that Macholl and Jack would come to blows?"

"No idea. You're the detective. You figure it out. Are we done?" Diane asked, as she stood, her awareness now registering that Jade stood a few feet off to her right.

Karen had tried the diplomatic approach, but Diane's abruptness pissed her off.

"No, we're not done. Sit down," Karen replied forcefully. "During the post-mortem, we identified long scratch marks across Jack's face. From what we can gather, that didn't happen at the restaurant."

"Well, perhaps Jack put up a fight just before someone shot him dead."

"Perhaps." Karen played along. "When I left here last time, I saw a male figure in one of the upstairs windows. Your son unless anyone else stays here?" Karen asked, glancing towards the hallway.

Diane shook her head. "No, it was just the three of us."

"From what I could see, your son had been in quite a violent altercation if his facial injuries are anything to go by. How did he come by those?"

Karen watched Diane's movements. They were small and subtle, alternating between wrapping her arms around her chest and curling a hand into a ball in her lap. Anxiety. Fear. Upset. Or all three.

Karen pushed for an answer. "Well? Did your son and Jack have a fight?"

Diane let out a nervous laugh. "Are you kidding? Why would my Ben and Jack fight? Besides, Ben is no match for Jack."

"Was there a disagreement or argument when you all returned from the restaurant?"

Diane shook her head. She wrung her hands faster.

Karen didn't let up.

"Because, when our forensic officers were examining the house, they found dozens of glass fragments in the other room."

Diane shrugged. "Maybe Jack dropped a glass at some point, and the shards were missed when cleaning up."

"Right…" Karen replied, not satisfied, her patience wearing thinner by the second.

Karen let the silence simmer for a few moments, knowing it would ratchet up Diane's anxiety. Karen wanted to stretch the boundaries of plausibility further.

"I'm wondering whether you and Jack were having a barney, Jack threw a glass, and Ben stepped in to protect you. Jack, in turn, attacked Ben. And then Ben later took revenge…?" Karen shrugged.

"No. No. No. It's not like that!" Diane screamed.

"What was it like then?" Karen pushed.

Diane bit her bottom lip and curled one fist into the palm of her other hand.

"Jack was angry when Dean turned up. Yes, it got heated. But Dean left before anything happened. And when we got home, Jack headed straight for the bar. I tried to calm him down, but he was going ballistic. He threw his whisky glass across the room. I didn't know it at the time, but Ben was standing outside in the hallway listening," Diane added, nodding towards the hallway.

Karen let her continue without interrupting. She glanced across at Jade, who scratched down some notes.

"Ben came in. He asked Jack to leave me alone. And Jack went mental. After he pushed me out of the way, I stumbled and fell to my knees. And when I looked up, Jack already had Ben pinned to the ground, beating the living daylights out of him. I thought he would kill him. So, I jumped on to Jack's back and tried to pull him off. He was too strong for me. I scratched his face with my nails. It's all I could think of doing. Then he turned on me."

Karen's mind switched back to the post-mortem and Taylor's face, before she tapped her own lip, regarding Diane's fat and swollen lip.

Diane nodded. "After that, Jack stormed out, and I helped take Ben upstairs and put him to bed. That was the last I saw of Jack until the following morning." She shuddered as the image of Jack's dead body resurfaced in her mind.

"What's the history between Dean and Jack?"

Diane lowered her head and stared at the ground.

Karen hissed out an exasperated sigh. "Diane, I will find out one way or another. You can make it easy for me or hard. But either way I will find out. So, stop pissing about."

"I don't know."

"Diane, I need you to understand that withholding any information that impedes our investigation is a criminal offence. Not wishing to add further difficulties to what you are already going through, if there's anything you know, then it would be in your best interests to tell me…"

Jade and Karen stared at Diane.

She could feel the heat from their stares, but Diane continued to hold her silence.

"We visited Dean Macholl." Karen waited a few seconds and noticed a flicker in Diane's eyelids. "Macholl holds a torch for you, doesn't he? He said you two had a history, and that you chose Jack over him when Dean asked you to make a choice."

The woman shook her head. "It wasn't like that. We were knocking around together. I think he was more serious about us than I was."

"Have you spoken to Dean Macholl since his release?"

"No."

"In the days before he was killed, were there any incidents, or threats to Jack's life?"

"No… not that I was aware of or saw."

"Okay, Diane. That's it for the moment. Thank you for your time."

"THIS IS GETTING thicker than a pea and potato soup."

Karen looked across as Jade drove off and smiled. "You come out with the weirdest stuff sometimes."

Jade continued to stare at traffic, her mouth wide in a pretend shock. "What…? Look at what we've got. We've got an ex-lover back on the scene, and a girlfriend and her son on the end of domestic violence. That's two powerful motives."

Karen agreed as she looked out of her side window. But something troubled her. Neither Macholl nor Diane behaved like murderers, but then *how* did murderers behave?

17

SKELTON TIPPED his head back into the pillow and drew in a large lungful from his cigarette. He stared at the ceiling, and locked his jaw several times, while breathing out, and watched the round circles of cigarette smoke rise above him. Each ring broke up the higher it rose, disappearing into emptiness.

The soft down pillows cushioned his head, and the cool silk sheets swathed his body as he relaxed after spending the last hour in bed. He had sneaked away from the office, needing to see her as much as she needed to see him. His body was warm and sticky, but it felt good to have been in Sally's company. Sex was always good with her. She was a passionate, domineering, demanding and strong woman in bed. She knew what she liked, and he loved that about her. Sally liked to lead. She was vocal and rough. In a way, they used each other. Neither wanted commitment, but both had their needs, urges and desires.

Sally lay beside him, scanning through messages on her two phones, oblivious to Skelton's presence.

"Sal, I need more credit. I'm due to be paid soon, so I can pay some of it back."

Sally tutted. "I hope you're not annoying the boys. Don't tell me… Steve and Terry knocked you back."

Skelton took another drag. "Yeah. But I thought you could have a word with them."

Sally didn't bother turning to look at him, choosing instead to continue browsing through her phone. "Well, there's your answer then. If they said no, then there's nothing I can do about it. They control the dens. Their rules."

"Yes," he spat. "But I thought you could put in a good word for me. Besides, we're…"

"We are what exactly? Lovers? In your dreams. This suits both of us. How much do you owe them?"

"Too much."

"That's not my problem, Pat. You've got yourself into this mess; you're big enough to get yourself out. You have a purpose. Don't ruin it. My brothers might work for me, but if you cross them, I won't be able to save you. This is a business, not a charity."

Sally threw back her sheet and stepped out of the bed. Her feet sunk into the thick, deep pile cream carpet in the spare bedroom. Even though Skelton visited her once or twice a week, she never took him to her own bed.

Skelton watched her pad across the floor. He lusted over her naked body as his eyes travelled up and down her form, before they settled on her firm breasts. A perfect 32C of silicone gel. She looked great for fifty-four. Sally was tall, around five foot eight, with a slim figure. She kept herself in shape, never overindulging in anything, and had never seen the inside of a gym even though a fully equipped one was downstairs at her disposal.

Despite having just had her, he wanted her again, and his groin twitched in response. She had short, blonde hair cut just beneath her ears, and unique, dark green eyes. Skelton loved her sharp nose and high cheekbones, and a strong bold voice that exuded authority, command and aggression. God, he admired her, and desired her more than any other woman. Whether it was her looks, or her presence and power, he wasn't sure, but suspected it was a powerful cocktail of both. She appeared untouchable and in control, traits he didn't possess.

She lit her own cigarette, and stood at the end of the bed with one hand on her hip, staring down her nose at Skelton. Her silk gown lay on the floor, and she appeared in no hurry to put it on.

"I've got a small shipment coming in. I need you to make sure that the coast is clear. It will be somewhere near the Wilson Industrial Estate. Do what you need to do. There's a package for you downstairs."

"Does it give me more credit?" he asked.

Sally blew out a long plume of smoke and stared at Skelton's naked top half. "No. It just stops you ending up in the Regent's Canal with a few breeze blocks tied to your ankles. You don't want to join a few others who've pissed us off in the past, do you?"

Skelton smiled, desperate to display an air of confidence. But inside, his stomach twisted in knots, and fear spread through him like an icy chill on a winter's day. He was on borrowed time, and he knew it.

Sally stubbed out her cigarette in the ashtray beside her. She leaned into him and kissed him hungrily, while one hand travelled down to his cock. She stroked his member, getting him firm, before she tightened her hand around his balls, and squeezed hard.

Skelton flinched and gasped.

"See yourself out. You've got five minutes," she stated, coldness lacing her tone. Sally rolled off the bed and headed towards the bedroom door. She left the room without glancing backwards, heading towards her own bedroom.

Skelton heard her door close. He stared at the ceiling and blew out his cheeks. He pulled his legs over the side of the bed and sat up, before looking around the bedroom. The room held an opulent feel. A tall bed, with a deep mattress, expensive sheets, and tasteful prints that caught the light from the small chandelier that took centre stage of the ceiling. He wondered how he had ended up like this at fifty-eight years old. He should have been retired by now, but he'd left a trail of destruction in his wake. Crimes had gone unsolved or overlooked, official stats had been manipulated, evidence had mysteriously disappeared, and he had turned a blind eye to criminal activity.

And for what?

After dressing, he made his way on to the landing, pausing for a moment to look at Sally's bedroom door. He pictured her inside, only a few steps away. But it could have been a mile. An eerie silence hovered over the house, as if it were uninhabited. Sally's kitchen was larger than the ground floor of most semi-detached houses. More expensive prints lined the hallway and the rooms downstairs. Chandeliers hung in every room, and with tall ceilings, every room had a sense of airiness and space.

Walking over to the kitchen table, he found the package. He picked it up and tossed it between his hands. *A decent amount*, he thought.

He exited through the back door, another condition Sally placed upon him. He had to make his way through the gardens, towards a small concealed exit in the far wall. He took one last look over his shoulder and considered that brief moment of pleasure he'd enjoyed, before walking back to his car parked more than half a mile away. Again, another condition Sally imposed upon him.

18

Karen tore bits from her sandwich and nibbled them as she stared at the incident board. She was a visual person and often spent hours staring at the data scribbled on the whiteboard. She wasn't a big one for holding mass team briefings unless there was something important to share, preferring instead for her officers to add to the board as the investigation proceeded, so news was visible for all to see.

Others on her team had added black-and-white stills of the various people present at the celebration dinner. Since their backgrounds had been checked and their alibis confirmed, a few had been crossed through with a red marker.

She had drawn a red circle around Macholl's picture and stared at the man's casual smile. There was something about him that was both mysterious and menacing. She had examined his file and despite his violent background, Macholl appeared to have turned a corner based on prison records requested from the Belgian authorities. Prison officials said he was a quiet, passive prisoner who served his time, and didn't get involved in any confrontations.

Nothing but circumstantial conjecture linked Macholl to the armed robbery where a cashier had been shot. Both Macholl and Taylor had been pulled in for questioning following a detailed investigation, but without concrete evidence linking them to the crime, they had been released. There was no DNA evidence, and detailed video analysis which mapped out the key characteristics of the three hooded men, did not tie either man to the crime.

Karen was certain there was something there. From what she had gathered, the two were intrinsically linked up until that robbery. And then something happened which led to Macholl disappearing and resurfacing in Belgium. Karen tapped the tip of the marker on her chin as her eyes darted around the board. She had added images of Diane Murphy, and her son Ben, both before and after the altercation with Taylor.

She now had three suspects.

"Guv."

Karen jumped when she heard Brad come up behind her. She had been so deep in thought that she hadn't heard him address her until he was inches away from her.

"Jesus, Brad, you nearly gave me a heart attack."

Brad dipped his head and glanced at Karen as he rubbed his neck. "Sorry, guv," he replied through a grimace.

"Neck giving you grief?"

He nodded as he massaged the muscles.

Karen glanced over her shoulder at his workstation and noticed the absence of an elevated stand for his PC monitor, and a chair with a higher back, both recommended by the occupational therapist.

Brad followed Karen's eyes and sighed. "I know. I've not chased her up yet, I will do. I promise. I've just got a lot on my mind."

Karen knew Brad faced his own emotional battles. He was a father of two young boys, but since splitting with his girlfriend, she hadn't given him an opportunity to see the boys, and always denied him access. Every time he asked to see them, she made excuses like the boys were busy, or they had homework to do, or were not well. If Brad turned up on her doorstep, she refused to answer the door.

Seeing the anguish etched on Brad's face only confirmed why she didn't want to take the risk of becoming a mother. She doubted she'd be a good wife, and the prospect of being a single parent horrified her. Those beliefs and her own childhood solidified her determination to remain single.

"Forensics have come back on Macholl's clothing and nail scrapings. I'm afraid it's a negative. There is no GS residue to suggest that he was in contact with a firearm."

"Bollocks."

It was news she didn't want to hear. A man of Macholl's reputation would have destroyed the clothes if he had shot Taylor. And of course, there was the question of the missing firearm. Macholl had been happy for Karen and Steve to search his small apartment on their visit. Either he was innocent or a bloody good actor.

Karen walked with Brad back to his desk, deep in thought. "Have you got anything else on Diane and her son Ben?"

Jade overheard the question and popped her head above her monitor. “I’ve been looking into that, guv. I’ve got two officers doing the legwork for us. Uniform had attended on three separate occasions during the last two years. Ben called once, and Diane called twice. Each time, because Jack was kicking off. No formal charges were made on our part, and Diane didn’t want to press charges. Jack had attacked Ben on two of those occasions, and on the third, he had attacked Diane.”

“And love is blind…” Karen muttered.

“Exactly, guv. On one occasion, the officers had to caution Ben for using threatening behaviour and language.”

The need to have another chat with Diane and Ben loomed on the horizon. But this time, with a search warrant.

WHILE THE TEAM busied themselves with the investigation, it afforded Karen an opportunity to process other things that were never far from her mind. She found herself back in the place where nine months ago her whole career had turned upside down. The evening rush hour traffic was dying down as she stood in Agar Grove in Camden. She walked up and down the road a few times before coming to a standstill at the exact spot where the ambush occurred. Her eyes scanned her surroundings before focusing on the ground in front of her. Her mind replayed the images of the growing pool of blood from the critically wounded police officer who lay near her feet. The viscous, red blood had rooted her to the spot.

It was as if someone had pressed play inside her mind as the sounds and sights came flooding back. The screams, the shouts, the gunshots. Everything swirled around her, just as they had on that fateful day.

She clamped her eyes tight desperate to block out the images that played out in slow motion. If anything, they amplified her experience, trapping her inside her mind and dragging her through every torturous second.

The shrinks had said that she would get over it, that time would heal the pain and anguish. How wrong they had been. The confusion was just as fresh, the events just as painful, and the anger just as raw. Not a day passed without her thinking about it, and for some reason this place kept drawing her back, as if revisiting it would help her to find the answers.

She clenched her fists, wanting to scream out loud. Most nights, alcohol helped to suppress the urges that threatened to engulf her. But nothing could take away the final images of Anne Woodland being dragged out the car by her hair, and the desperate, silent plea for help etched on her face, as she stared in Karen's direction. She had watched an innocent person go to their death, and had frozen through fear, unable to respond… she hadn't been able to save her.

Completely helpless.

Failure had never sat comfortably with her. She chose instead to work harder than anyone else around her. But on that day in Camden, she had failed.

She walked the streets for the next hour or two, oblivious to those who passed by her, trapped in her own thoughts and the whirlwind of emotions that smothered her.

She needed a drink, a proper drink, one that would blot out everything.

19

THE FIRST SIGNS of light pierced Karen's eyeballs like laser beams as she flickered awake. She'd paid thirty pounds for an Uber to get her back to Epping. After putting her key in the door at three a.m., she'd dropped her bag in the hallway and collapsed into bed, fully clothed.

Now, she rubbed her eyes and stared up at the ceiling. Licking her dry lips, she tried to swallow the sticky mess of mucus that had collected in the back of her throat. She rolled on to one side and pulled the duvet over her head, a muffled groan signalling her displeasure and lack of sleep.

"Why do I keep doing this?" she muttered, as she threw off her duvet twenty minutes later. She made her way to the kitchen, and flicked on the kettle, before pouring herself a glass of water. The liquid slipped down her throat, jolting her senses, and etched away at the dehydration that had left her with a parched mouth, and a dull, heavy head.

While the kettle boiled, Karen stripped down and stepped slowly into the shower, her toes flinching as they touched the chilled ceramic floor. Turning the water on high, she let it beat over her head in steamy rivulets. She closed her eyes to the water as the heat soaked into her skin before leaning against the cool tiles as her weak and tired legs threatened to buckle.

Her thoughts turned towards where she had ended up last night, a random bar in one of the backstreets of Camden. Flashbacks darted in and out of her awareness. As the night had worn on, she had caught Neil's attention. She couldn't remember much of the conversation, but they had spent a few hours chatting, egging each other on to see how many tequila slammers they could take. It was the break she needed, neither of them touching on their personal circumstances. Just two adults, letting off steam.

She smiled to herself as she recalled ending up at Neil's apartment. They had ripped their clothes off in the doorway as he fumbled with the key. Vivid recollections flooded her awareness of the sex that followed before they'd even made it to the bedroom. It was a release that her mind and body craved.

There were no expectations, and that suited Karen. She had convinced herself a long time ago that she wasn't the relationship type. Being a die-hard commitment-phobe, she had thrown all her energy into her career. Family life growing up had been good, but events in her childhood with her younger sister had left an indelible mark which had frightened her ever since.

THE POLICE OFFICER stood to one side as Karen and Jade breezed through the front gates of Taylor's house. Two squad cars followed Jade's car, and their arrival didn't go unnoticed as the odd bystander and the last few remaining journalists snapped away on their cameras.

Karen exited the car and marched towards the front door, not looking back to see where the uniformed officers were. She knocked hard, and then rang the doorbell, before knocking once more. If the intention was to startle Diane, and catch her off guard, Karen had achieved that aim.

Annoyance and confusion flashed in Diane's eyes as she opened the door.

"You're having a laugh, ain't you? You were only here a few hours ago. Are you trying to harass me or something? I've lost Jack, and you can think of nothing better to do than keep knocking on my door. You should be out there looking for whoever did it." Diane fumed, jabbing a finger towards the main road.

"We are, Diane. But we're following several lines of investigation. Where's Ben?"

The question took Diane by surprise.

"Um… um. He's upstairs in his room. Why?"

Karen brushed past Diane, ignoring her question, and the remonstrating that followed.

Jade pulled Diane to one side and presented her with a search warrant. She also explained that because Ben had made threats to kill Taylor, Ben needed questioning as part of the investigation.

Once inside, uniformed officers moved off in different directions, their heavy footsteps echoing around the cavernous hallway. Karen had given a remit instructing them in what they needed to search for.

Karen was in no mood to play games. A thumping headache and just a few hours of sleep had left her grizzly and impatient. She had made her way to the first-floor landing, where she opened each door until she found Ben's bedroom.

He sat on his bed with his pillows stuffed behind him, and his laptop resting on his legs. Plugged in with a set of headphones he hadn't heard the commotion downstairs, and jerked when Karen poked her head around the door. He yanked off his headphones and stared at her with a startled look on his face.

"Who are you?" he asked, his voice cracking in fear.

Karen pulled out her warrant card. "Detective Inspector Heath. I'm investigating the death of Jack Taylor. I'd like you to come down to the station with us to answer a few questions."

Ben ran his hand through his dark brown hair and swallowed hard. "Why me?"

"I can explain all of that when you come down to the station. Let's just say new evidence has come to light which requires us to have a chat."

Karen noticed the injuries to his face were far worse than she had first thought.

"Where's my mum?" he demanded as he pushed his laptop to one side, and scrambled off the bed to make his way towards the door.

Karen rolled her eyes and stepped to one side to allow him to pass as he shot by her. She turned and followed just a few steps behind. "Slow down, Ben. Your mum isn't going anywhere in a hurry."

She caught up with him downstairs just as he reached his mum.

"What's going on, Mum?" he asked, searching her eyes for an answer.

"It's okay, baby. It's just standard bullshit. The Old Bill are scratching around trying to find anyone to blame, and we are the easiest targets because we were the closest to Jack. Isn't that right, *Inspector*…" Diane glared Karen.

"You can say whatever you want, Diane, but new information has surfaced and we need Ben to explain a few things to us."

"Is he under arrest?"

"No. He's helping us with our enquiries. He will be cautioned at the station, but he will be free to go whenever he wants. And you are more than welcome to arrange legal representation for him, or we can arrange for a duty solicitor, should you think either are necessary?"

Diane scowled at Karen, but Karen held her steely gaze, neither woman willing to back down.

Diane relented, turning to Ben. "It will be fine, babe. If they give you any grief, you call me, and I'll arrange for our brief to come and sort it."

Ben shot Karen a cold stare before he turned and made his way to the car outside accompanied by Jade.

The angry glare was just the start, then came the strut, the slamming and the clipped words as he disappeared.

Karen offered Diane a sarcastic smile. “Thank you for your time, Diane. My other officers will remain while they continue their search. I’ve asked them to contact me should you impede them.”

20

BEN CAST a lonely figure sitting in the interview room. He sat at a small table which had four chairs around it. A black tape recorder machine sat to one side of the table. He tapped furiously on the side of his chair as he slouched back, and stared up at the ceiling before blowing out his cheeks.

"Bored, bored, bored," he muttered.

Karen watched him from the observation room. A small CCTV camera mounted high on the wall offered anyone watching a clear view into any interview.

"How do you want to play this, boss?" Jade asked.

Karen sighed. She hadn't eaten or drunk anything all day, and still suffered the effects of dehydration. Her head felt heavy and her body felt sluggish. She was getting too old for this, and at that moment she groaned. Her friend Debbie had texted her this morning about a night out in the City, and Karen had forgotten to reply earlier. She'd do it once the interview ended.

"We need to explore the death threats. I don't give a crap he's been beaten up. That doesn't afford him any slack. We stick to finding out how much he hated Jack."

KAREN HELD off for as long as she could before interviewing Ben to unsettle him. But she had another reason to delay. She wanted to give the police officers searching Taylor's residence enough time to find anything linking Ben to the investigation. News had come through that the search team had seized clothes Ben was wearing on the night of Taylor's murder. The discovery of several mobile phones in Ben's bedroom gave Karen her first breakthrough.

Armed with the information, Karen and Jade stepped into the interview suite.

If their arrival was meant to panic him, it had the opposite effect. He continued to slouch but lowered his head as in prayer. When Karen called his name, his gaze rose slowly to view the two officers.

Karen switched on the tape recorder, and went through the time, date, officers present, and standard caution.

As Jade readied herself with her notepad and pen, Karen took a few moments to flick through her case file. The silence intentional on her part.

"Those are nasty injuries, Ben. Did you get those seen to?" Karen asked.

Ben shook his head, continuing to hold his stare.

"Ben, we need you to verbalise your answers for the benefits of the tape," Karen requested, pointing towards the black tape recorder.

"No." Ben sighed.

"Your mum said Jack attacked you. He must have been upset to do that to you?"

"Listen. Why are you asking me that? You…" Ben gestured in Jade's direction, "already know from when you took my swab and took a statement from me. It's no secret that wanker did it to me."

Karen nodded. "I guess it must have left you feeling… angry?"

"You get used to it. Jack's gone. And that's the main thing. He can't hurt me, or my mum."

Karen's eyes narrowed. "You sound pleased that he's dead?"

"Of course, I am. He made Mum's life a misery. He made *our* lives a misery. And whenever I stood up for her, he had a pop at me. She was scared shitless of him. She once said she'd walk away from him if he ever hit me again… but she never did."

"And why's that?"

"Because he would have come after her. She knew too much about his business."

"So, it's convenient for you and your mum he's gone? You both get to inherit a sizeable chunk of his fortune."

"Look. I know you're trying to get me to say I killed Jack. But I didn't. I can't even remember falling asleep; I was in that much pain. If you think for one minute I had the strength to crawl out of my bed, find a gun, walk down to the end of the garden, and shoot him, then you must be on a different planet."

Karen changed tactics. "One of my officers discovered a message on a mobile phone they retrieved from your bedroom. It matches the exact message received on the phone given to Dean Macholl. You know the one, Ben… The one inviting him to Jack Taylor's birthday party."

She let the bombshell settle for a few minutes.

Ben shrugged his shoulders. "So?"

Karen crossed her arms and laid on a mock look of confusion. "I don't understand this. Why would you send a message to someone who has had no contact with Taylor as far as we know in the past five years? And more to the point, someone who wasn't welcome?"

The slightest of smirks cracked on Ben's face.

"Mum said Jack and Dean had fallen out, and that we were not to mention Dean's name in the house. All I knew was that Jack was glad that Dean was out of the picture. So, I couldn't think of a better way to ruin his birthday party."

"So, is that why you've threatened to kill him in the past?"

Ben's eyes twitched, as he sensed where the conversation was headed. "Hold on, hold on. I know what you're trying to do. Just because I threatened to kill him, it doesn't mean I did. I wanted him out of our lives. I didn't kill him; I swear. He hurt my mum. She used to be fun. Now she's a nervous wreck and looking over her shoulder."

Karen leant into the table and placed her elbows on the surface. "Listen, we're just trying to find out what happened to Taylor. You and your mum have both been through a tough time, but that was your mum's choice. But my question is why did you contact Dean Macholl? Did you hope he'd kill Jack?"

Ben glanced around the room. He knew they were scrutinising his every move, and analysing his every word. He reached forward and grabbed the paper cup. The few sips of cold water moistened his dry mouth.

"Whether or not you know it, there's a lot of beef between Jack and Dean. I ain't telling you nothing that's not already known on the street." He gestured, throwing a thumb towards the window. "Jack was behind the raid on the bookies that went Pete Tong. And Jack spread the word on the street that Dean was the one who'd shot the cashier."

"And did he?"

Ben shook his head and bowed. "Jack did it. I heard him tell my mum."

Karen suspended the interview.

"What do you think?" Jade asked, as they loitered in the corridor outside.

"Unless we find any gunshot residue on his clothes, then it's hard to link him to Taylor's murder. There's no DNA evidence linking him to the crime scene. Other than a vile hatred of the man, and a desperate need to protect his mum, we haven't got enough to hold or charge him for now."

"Shall I release him for the time being, boss?"

Karen nodded and swallowed her frustration. She left Jade to wrap up the interview and see Ben outside while she headed up to the canteen which overlooked the front of the building.

She stared out to the busy street below and watched as the taxis weaved in and out of the stationary delivery vans. Cyclist couriers whistled and sped into oncoming traffic. Office workers poured out of the glass monoliths that reached towards the sky. Everyday life continued all around her.

This was her life, dealing with low life scum, day in and day out. Listening to their lies, their deceit and unwrapping their motives.

She sipped her coffee and scrunched her face as the bitterness hit the back of her throat. "This is gross," she fumed, and then she froze.

Karen left the cup by the window, and raced through the building, taking the steps as fast as she could. "Get out of my way," she shouted as she charged through officers coming the other way, much to their consternation, before she exploded out of the front door. She glanced across the road but couldn't see them. "Shit!" she shouted, as her eyes tracked up and down the road. Had her eyes played tricks on her? Had dehydration and fatigue made her see things that weren't there?

No, she was adamant. She was sure she had seen Ben leave the front of the building and cross over the road to meet Dean Macholl.

21

THE WINDOWS HAD STEAMED up long ago. The distinct smell of vinegar soured the air as they both picked through their portion of fish and chips. It wasn't much, but it was food, and Molly was grateful for that. They sat in silence, each with their own thoughts, as grime music pulsated through the speakers in the doors.

Molly lightened the mood by drawing a smiley face on her passenger window. If she had one wish, she wanted a smiley face like that all the time. She washed down a mouthful of food with a gulp of Tango and burst out laughing when a burp escaped. Harry turned and smiled at her. She wished she could tell Harry everything. About how frightened she was of Finchy and the way he touched her, and his threats of gang-raping her as an initiation ceremony. But Harry took on everyone's problems. Ben always confided in him, she always moaned to him, and yet, Harry had no one *he* could lean on.

She felt his pain, and his anger. Harry didn't have family, but then again, she knew that family wasn't always the answer. He never spoke about his mum. Molly knew that as he grew up, it was just him and his mum, until she died. She learnt not to ask or probe too much. On the few occasions she'd asked, her questions were met with a wall of silence, and an anger in his eyes. However, as they got to know each other, he started to reveal small details, the reasons why he did what he did. But Harry was tough, one of life's survivors. And whenever she or Ben moaned to him, he would always reassure them both that everything would be okay, and he would take care of them.

The thought of going back home and checking on her mum crossed her mind, but she assumed her mum would be sprawled out across the sofa, her eyes dancing and her mind floating in a drug-induced state.

Scrunching up his chip paper, Harry wiped his mouth with the back of his hand. "That was pukka. That filled the gap. What do you want to do now?"

Molly wasn't sure. "I don't wanna go home at the moment. Can we drive for a bit?"

Harry nodded, winked, and squeezed her thigh. "Anything for you." He turned the key in the ignition, and revved his car a few times, before dropping off the handbrake and wheel-spinning away.

Today of all days, she could have done without this. She had texted Debbie not long after finishing her interview with Ben, and had confirmed, with reluctance, that she would meet her at a bar near Liverpool Street. Sleep deprived, hungry, and in a foul mood, the thought of standing in a bar filled with thirty-somethings, City professionals with big egos, and even bigger wallets, wasn't something she looked forward to.

She tried to convince herself that there was still time to back out. It would be easy to fob off Debbie with a text saying that she was manic at work, and would be stuck in the office for a few more hours… blah-blah. She had done that a few times in the past, and they had been genuine excuses, but her mind fought with her conscience as she gritted her teeth and drew in air. *Go in, turn around, go in, turn around, don't let her down, you'll regret it, stop being so selfish, I need something to distract my mind.*

Worried that people were looking at her as she stood in silence staring at the doors to the bar like some weirdo, she pulled her shoulders back, took a deep breath and pushed through.

A thousand conversations echoed around the bar and hit her in the face. It was a long, dark bar, situated opposite Liverpool Street station in Central London. The Railway Tavern provided a convenient stop-off point for commuters who wanted a quick drink before heading home. The familiar smell of ale and pub grub wafted around her as Karen squeezed through the thick gathering of bodies as she inched towards a bar. The men were in Chinos and open-necked shirts, their sleeves rolled up towards their elbows, the women dressed in dreary grey and black, standard fashion for working in the City.

She found Debbie by the bar, chatting to a group of City types. Raucous laughter exploded amongst them, and for a moment she felt awkward about joining them. The thought of the conversation stopping, and half a dozen pairs of eyes training on her, left her uncomfortable. It wasn't too late for her to backtrack and bail out because Debbie hadn't turned to see her yet.

"Sod it," Karen muttered.

She tapped Debbie on the shoulder, and her friend turned to greet her with a big smile, her eyes widening in excitement. Debbie squealed something incoherent, her words lost in the bubble of noise around them. The next few moments happened so quickly that Karen couldn't take much in.

Debbie spun back around and introduced Karen to the group she had been talking to. The men smiled, and nodded politely. She caught one or two of them glancing at their phones but using it as a ploy to look her up and down.

Why did men do that?

"Oh my God, it's been so long. How have you been?" Debbie asked, as she leant against the bar and waved a tenner to catch a bartender's attention. "What do you want?"

"Just a Diet Coke. I think I'm a bit hung-over from last night."

Debbie stared at her friend, a mixture of horror and annoyance distorting her features. "No way. I've not seen you in weeks, and you want a soft drink? There is no way I'm letting my mate have one tonight. Besides, give it an hour, and this lot will be buying the drinks." She nodded back in the group's direction.

Karen really wasn't in the mood for this. Normally, she wouldn't have hesitated, but men in general were grating on her last nerve.

"Okay then, get me a Kopparberg cider."

"Flavour?"

"Strawberry and lime, please."

"That's my girl," Debbie replied as she screamed along the bar to get some attention.

Debbie was a little shorter than Karen, vivacious and bubbly. She kept her bleached blonde hair long, and always in a ponytail that framed her dark brown eyes, and blemish-free skin. Karen admired Debbie's toned body, the result of sweat and effort in the gym five days a week before work. She was attractive and rarely short of male company. The men loved her, and she loved the attention.

They first met when they were doing their time at Hendon training college. Debbie did five years in the Met before she resigned, deciding that it wasn't the career for her. She took a job as a PA for an insurance firm in a glass building in the City known as The Gherkin.

"Shall we go back and chat to those guys?" Debbie asked. "You never know where it might lead? Wink wink, say no more!" Debbie nudged Karen in the ribs and shrugged her shoulders.

If Karen considered herself bad, she knew Debbie was worse. Debbie had often referred to Karen as her wing-woman, but on this occasion, the thought of copping off with another bloke didn't appeal to her. Truth be told, she wanted the one drink, and then head home to feed Manky, grab a shower, and crawl under her duvet. Sleep was calling her name.

"Listen, I can't stay for long. I've got a massive case on at the moment. And I need to go home and do a bit of work. You know what it's like." Karen hated lying, but she hoped

Debbie couldn't see through her weak attempt at an excuse.

Debbie pulled a face of disappointment. "Oh, come on, we hardly get out. You're beginning to sound like an old woman. Next you'll be telling me you need to go home to feed the cat and put on your slippers."

Debbie wasn't far from the truth, and Karen cringed.

"I'll stay for one or two more drinks, but then I really must go. I'm sorry. But as soon as this case is out of the way, I promise that we'll go out, and I'll pay."

Debbie smiled before they continued to catch up on each other's lives, and their work. Because of Karen's work, she couldn't say too much, so let Debbie do most of the talking. And Debbie loved to talk. For the next hour she talked about her work, her bosses, the people she fancied at work, and her plans for a holiday to Bali next year. Karen nodded all the way through, adding a few oohs, and aahs for effect.

Karen swigged more cider and felt herself relax. The tension she carried in her chest eased, and she felt the muscles in her shoulders loosen.

"So, you haven't told me yet. Is there a man in your life?" Debbie was sniffing the titbits of gossip.

Karen shook her head. "You know me. I'm too much of a heartbreaker. The last thing I want is a bloke giving me puppy dog eyes. Sod that."

"God, you're a harsh woman. I swear you get worse by the year. You sure you're not knocking on the door of *the big change*?"

Karen pulled a face. "Oh my God, how old do you think I am? I'm not redundant in that department you know. I still love a good shag. But when it suits me."

"I'm sure you used to be a bloke in a previous life. You are definitely a love them and leave them merchant."

Karen and Debbie both laughed as Karen agreed it wasn't far from the truth.

Debbie made her excuses for a few minutes while she visited the loo and came back to tell Karen that the men had invited them on to a club.

Seeing it as a perfect opportunity to make her excuses, she tapped the dial of her watch with one finger and told Debbie that she needed to get back.

Debbie accepted that with reluctance but urged Karen to make time for her as soon as possible. Karen agreed, and told Debbie to be careful, and to call her this evening if she needed bailing out. Debbie appreciated the sentiment but promised she would be okay.

With that, they both hugged, and Karen left. Stepping out on to the pavement, she blew out her cheeks. She felt bad for leaving Debbie, but there was so much on her mind that she knew she wouldn't be able to relax and enjoy the rest of the evening. She walked across the road to the station and headed down towards the Central Line platform to get her train back to Epping. With luck, she would be home and in bed before midnight.

22

THE NOISE ENGULFED HER, completely capturing her brain, rendering any logical thought or conclusion impossible. Her body jerked as she fell. Her head hit the carpet with a thud as her body followed a second later. The force of hitting the floor winded her for a moment. Three bottles of cider had left her dead to the world, her mouth feeling like the rug by her door, bristly and rough.

Her phone rattled as it bounced across the glass surface of her coffee table.

The cogs in her brain spun, making sense of things, desperate to catch up with her movements. *This is so not my bedroom.* It took a few more moments for her to realise that she was on the floor in the lounge, and somehow, she must've fallen asleep on the sofa not long after getting in.

She jolted awake and rose to her knees, hanging on to the sofa for support, as she glanced around in the darkness, the only illumination from the screen of her mobile phone.

"I'm here; I'm around. Who is it?" she muttered wildly to herself.

She grabbed her mobile, desperate to stop the ringing, as it pierced her brain. With one eye open, the other reluctant to join in, she hit the green icon before closing her eyes again.

"Yeaaah… Karen here." Her voice was harsh and gravelly.

"Sorry to disturb you, guv. This is Duty Sergeant Atwood. I tried DCI Skelton first as the SIO, but…" there was a hesitation in the man's voice, "but the DCI told me to call you, and said in no uncertain terms, not to call him again."

Karen massaged her temples as she listened to the sergeant. *That sounds like Skelton, only dealing with police business when it suits him. Tosser*, sprang to mind.

"What's the time?"

"It's four forty a.m., guv."

"Oh my God." She groaned. She had been asleep for four hours.

"I'm sorry to wake you up, guv, but I need you and your team to attend a scene as soon as possible."

The sense of urgency in the sergeant's voice brushed away the final cobwebs of sleep as she narrowed her eyes and continued to listen.

"Our officers were called to the apartment of Dean Macholl. There's been a shooting and a fatality."

"Fatality?"

"Yes, guv. Dean Macholl was the fatality."

The news sent Karen's mind into a wild vortex as theories were thrown out of the window, and fresh ideas were thrown into the mix. The alarming news extinguished a major line of investigation in the space of a few hours. And yet she'd just seen him less than twenty-four hours earlier. Living and breathing, stood across the road from the station.

Karen cut the call, telling the sergeant to alert the rest of her team.

She ran to the bathroom, and leant into the mirror. Itchy and bloodshot eyes, and a white-furred tongue greeted her.

"God, I look like rat shit. In fact, rat shit probably smells better than me," she continued, as she cupped her hands over her mouth. She puffed an exhale before sniffing the air, and screwing up her face.

Flicking on the basin tap, Karen splashed handfuls of cold water on her face, the chill jolting her senses, and awakening her. She glanced up towards the mirror, but was disappointed, as the same tired face and small eyes stared back at her. "Sod it. It will have to do."

Karen ran a brush through her hair, doing her best to flatten it out, the bristles catching on the knots. She then rummaged around in her cupboard for something quick to throw on. A pair of jeans and a long-sleeved T-shirt would have to do. A pair of white, grubby Converse trainers finished off her urban chick look.

At this time of the morning, the Central Line wouldn't be running. Despite her reluctance, she jumped into her Mini Paceman. Epping to Shoreditch was almost an hour, but with empty roads and sunrise, she hoped to be there in a little over thirty minutes.

THE FAMILIAR LINE of blue and white police tape confirmed her destination as she drove down Columbia Road. When she had last been here, she'd discovered that the road played host to one of London's most visually appealing markets. Columbia Road flower market took place every Sunday with overflowing bucketfuls of beautiful flowers, houseplants, herbs, bulbs and shrubs.

On a day like this, that natural wonder seemed a distant contrast to the gloom and sombreness of the street as she pulled up behind a long line of squad cars. The garish yellow façade of the apartment block did little to lighten the mood. Several officers milled around, keeping early morning spectators at arm's length.

Karen signed into the scene log, and grabbed herself a white paper suit, gloves, and blue foot coverings before making her way into Macholl's apartment block.

Steve and Brad were already on site, standing by the front door to Macholl's apartment, and talking with one of the SOCOs.

"What have we got, gents?" Karen asked as she unzipped her suit and stepped into it, pulling one arm through and then the other before zipping it up.

Brad looked at his notes to double-check what he had written. "Several neighbours called about two seventeen a.m., after hearing what they thought was a gunshot or car back-firing. One or two of the residents looked out to see a figure disappearing through the gates and turning right before making their way down the road at speed."

"Description?"

Brad shook his head. "Nothing, guv, other than a dark figure. We can't confirm if it was male, female or Quasimodo." He tutted.

Karen rolled her eyes, both at the lack of description, and Brad's feeble attempt at injecting humour into the situation. "Macholl?"

"The pathologist has confirmed a single gunshot to the chest. More than likely penetrated the heart."

"Is Wainwright still here?"

Brad shook his head. "No, boss. The pathologist has been and gone. He said he would catch up with you later. I think he was going straight from here down to the Thames. River Police have pulled out a body."

"So, first Taylor, and now Macholl. Both with a single gunshot wound. Is this the start of a vendetta or turf war?" Steve speculated.

"Your guess is as good as mine, Steve. Okay, let's take a look," Karen said as she stepped through the doorway.

As she made her way into the bedroom the small apartment was as she remembered. Since it wasn't big enough to accommodate all of them, Steve and Brad paused at the door, while Karen joined two SOCOs who were continuing their investigation. It was a scene she was all too familiar with but had never got used to. The smell was subtle and less repulsive than the ones that clung to her at the mortuary.

The added odour of cigarettes hung in the air. As far as she knew, Macholl didn't smoke.

She paused for a moment as she watched the figure of Macholl lying slumped to one side of the sofa. He was naked other than a pair of boxer shorts. Something about him had captured her initial interest. Maybe it was his swagger, or his charisma and confidence. But she felt a slight hint of sadness as she stared at his crumpled form.

Not wishing to disturb the scene any further, Karen took a few moments to glance around the small room. She noticed the rumpled bed linens, and two indentations in the mattress. There were also two wine glasses, one empty, the other containing the remnants of what appeared to be red wine.

Macholl had company.

Karen turned towards the female forensic officer who was documenting the evidence they had gathered in clear plastic bags. "Have you found anything of interest?"

The SOCO glanced up and nodded. She spoke from behind her face mask, the fabric puffing in and out as she spoke. "We recovered hair samples from both pillows. There are a couple of short strands, which possibly belonged to the deceased. But I also recovered two longer brown hair samples from one pillow. They are probably near ten to twelve inches long. There are also some stains on the bed sheets. We'll examine them for DNA."

"Anything else?"

The SOCO held up several clear evidence bags and passed them in Karen's direction.

Karen examined the contents of each bag. Each one contained a handwritten letter. The dates on each letter were several months apart, and were written from a female perspective. She would examine them later, but what drew her attention to each letter was the signature. Just the initial D, followed by a single kiss underneath.

Karen looked up from the evidence bags and glanced around the room. Macholl's clothes lay in a pile to one side of his bed. She imagined he had climbed into that side of the bed, and his guest had joined him on the other side. But her eyes were drawn to the bedside table and a thick, sturdy book that sat by the lamp.

"Is it okay if I head over there?" Karen asked, jabbing her finger towards the bedside table.

The SOCO glanced over her shoulder and nodded.

As Karen got nearer to the table she realised the thick book was in fact a copy of the Bible.

Macholl, religious? I didn't expect that.

It was open, and she leaned in to take a closer look at a page that had been circled in red. The book hadn't been dusted for prints, so she didn't touch it, but read out the section circled.

Deuteronomy 32:35

It is mine to avenge; I will repay.

In due time their foot will slip;

their day of disaster is near

this and their doom rushes upon them.

23

THE THOUGHT of crawling under her desk and falling asleep appealed to her more than sifting through the case file.

Too little sleep, an empty stomach, and remnants of alcohol left her with a growling and burning stomach that distracted her from the task in hand. Part of her was preoccupied with the ambush eight months ago. The haunting memory lingered, never far from her thoughts and would often side-track her from important work. Shaking her head, and thumping her desk with a clenched fist, she jolted herself back into the present.

Forensics would wrap up their search of Macholl's apartment soon. Even though ballistics wouldn't have access to the bullet until after the post-mortem, Karen would work on the assumption that the results would reveal the same firearm used to kill Taylor. That they were associates, and killed within days of each other, made it more of a certainty in her mind.

Steve tapped on her open door, and hovered in the doorway, waiting to be called in. Karen waved him in as she clicked through various emails, deciding which to keep and which to send to the bin.

"I've got an update for you, boss." Steve grabbed a seat, straightening his tie, even though it didn't need straightening.

The action bought a slight smile to Karen's face. It didn't matter where Steve was, or what he was doing, his appearance came first. He was the smartest, and snazziest dresser in MIT, and every time he walked into another station, officers would give him a second look. Pencil-thin ties, small collars, and neatly pressed white shirts were his trademark. Sometimes his trousers looked as if they'd been sprayed on.

"We had officers doing door-to-door enquiries. As we know, several residents heard what they thought was a loud pop and put it down to a car backfiring shortly after two a.m. However, we've also got one witness who saw someone leaving around one a.m. This resident was just going to sleep when they heard the electronic release on the front door to the block. She's an old dear and likes to be nosey. Her admission, not mine. Anyway, she looked out and saw someone walking away from the front door and making their way towards the main road."

"Description?" Karen asked, making notes on her pad.

"Female. Average height, dark hair, wearing a long coat, and high heels. The witness distinctly remembered the sound of heels clicking across the path."

The timings didn't work for Karen. But that wasn't to say that whoever it was didn't return. One thing was certain,

Macholl had female company just hours before someone killed him.

"What do you reckon, boss? Do you think the same person returned an hour later and shot him?"

Karen tapped the end of her pen on the desk. "The letters we found were signed with the initial D. My hunch is that it was Diane. I think she's got too much to lose by going back and killing Macholl. Besides, I'm not sure what the motive would be. If Diane thought he was responsible for Taylor's death, then it could be a simple act of revenge. I wouldn't put it past her to get access to a firearm."

"But if it was the same firearm used to kill Taylor, then I don't understand her motive for killing both?"

"Me, neither. Okay. Thanks, Steve."

Steve stood, and straightened out the creases in his trousers before turning to leave. Karen watched him but averted her gaze when she found her eyes tracking down his body. She clenched her teeth. *God, what is wrong with me. I'm his boss, not a forty-something cougar.*

Karen was waning. Hunger assaulted her so she couldn't think straight. One minute she was focused on the case, the next, thinking about motives, before moving on to men and carnal instincts.

She pushed her chair back and arched her spine to relieve the tension. She was fast approaching not having eaten for twenty-four hours and needed food. It was a common problem. Officers went for most of their shift without eating as they became absorbed in their cases, pushing food to the back of their minds. And then they would resort to fast food binges while they continued to work. An endless stream of moped riders arrived at the front door, delivering kebabs, Chinese and pizzas.

Karen needed something more substantial which would help her survive the whole day. With Macholl's post-mortem scheduled for later in the day, she would rather eat now and allow it to settle. Wainwright had a habit of making her feel uncomfortable as he carved his way through the cadavers.

She headed for the local Tesco Metro, and settled for a boring chicken pasta, a pack of fruit salad, and coconut water.

"What a glorious life I lead, a meal for one yet again," she said as she sat in her office and stared at the delectable feast that did little to excite her.

Karen envied the life that Steve led. He had two passions in life, his motorbike and his car. She had seen his bike frequently, but only seen his car once. It was his pride and joy. He had a genuine Mustang, the exact model that Steve McQueen had driven. She couldn't remember much of the detail, but the words *Bullitt* and Highland green sprang to mind. Oh, that and the price tag. He had paid forty thousand pounds. She wasn't sure where he got the money to afford his expensive lifestyle, perhaps a rich aunt or uncle, or some inheritance, but it wasn't from a police salary. Every officer she knew struggled to get by on the money they earned. She was curious to know, just to be nosey more than anything else, but had never asked.

God she was envious of him. A carefree life with some simple pleasures. And what did she have? An apartment in the middle of Essex, a moggy and a fridge full of wine. Her thoughts turned to her sister. Guilt flashed through her mind as she stared at her mobile phone, willing herself to pick it up, but something stopped her. Was it really guilt? Or was it out of sight out of mind? But that would be worse, surely? Maybe it was denial or the fact that if she kept herself busy long enough, she wouldn't have to think about her.

24

THE INNER CITY grew around him like an uncontrolled spawning of concrete and metal alleyways and roads that led in every direction. The only splash of colour in the grime came from the lurid graffiti and the pavements that were littered with drugs paraphernalia. From every covered doorway came the dejected stares of men and women in their pathetic cardboard sleeping bags. From upper windows came the boom of music and a fusion of curry and cannabis smells. The hookers stalked the streets in their skimpy outfits and high boots looking for work, their drug-addled bodies as thin as pins, their cheekbones jutting out through pallid skin.

Here he could be anyone, or perhaps no one at all, and that suited him. He could move in the shadows, street to street, ducking in doorways, and darting around the web of council housing estates that sat shoulder to shoulder with Victorian terraced town houses.

Shoreditch was a melting pot of diverse cultures, the wealthy and the poor, the trendy urbanites and the working class.

Skelton didn't want to know, or care. They were scum. Filthy, desperate scum who would stab their own mother in the back for a lump of crack. As a bobby on the beat, he loved the area, and people knew where they stood. There was good and bad. That was it. Nothing more complicated. It was a patch he'd grown up in. His dad and grandad were in the police. His dad was in the flying squad in the late fifties. Skelton was in his teens at the time and joined the police at eighteen.

His dad was old school. The old flying squad sent chilling shards of fear through the criminal underworld. A punch and a whack with a pickaxe handle were just as effective as a truncheon. And Skelton represented a dying breed. Gone were the days where CID and criminals stood by side in shady backstreet pubs, swapping information and keeping tabs on each other.

Now it was procedures, PACE, digital voice recorders, CCTV, and forensics that led the way.

Skelton dipped back into a doorway and blew out a plume of cigarette smoke that swirled and hung in the air in front of his face.

People walked past him, hurrying to wherever they needed to go, flowing like rivers, never stopping for obstacles but skirting around them. A few cast a disparaging look. He retaliated with his own steely stare that made them glance away in fear and uncertainty.

He waited, as he always did. The man he was meeting was always late, no doubt holed up in some pit or drug den, getting off his face. He was a liability when like that, but Skelton needed him, and knew how to manipulate the man's weaknesses.

Skelton glanced at his watch. Eighteen minutes and counting. He clenched his teeth in frustration. Checking the street in both directions, he saw the man bumble along, glancing into each car as he passed. Skelton could accurately read every stilted action. He was looking for anything of value. A satnav, handbag, phone, or an expensive scarf. Small items were easy to flog down the local pub. He made a few hundred pounds a week doing just that. His work for Skelton topped that up.

Skelton stepped out of the doorway long enough for the man to see him, before taking a step back into the shadows.

The man crossed the road and joined him.

"What's happening, man?"

Skelton studied the man for a few moments. He called him Lizard, and for a reason. The man had chronic eczema. His skin was scabby, red and peeling. His face looked like it was moulting. Skelton sneered at him, wondering what he might catch if he touched him.

"I've got a job for you," Skelton muttered.

Lizard's face lit up. The prospect of earning cash fired up his senses. His dark and dirty, bloodshot eyes shifted wildly in excitement. He tucked his hands in his pockets and pulled his shoulders in tight to his ears.

"Always happy to help, you know me. What's the dealio?"

"I need you to create a distraction tonight. Do you know Shadbolts, the timber place?"

Lizard narrowed his eyes, and stared towards the sky, trying to place the location. He took a few moments, but then certainty appeared in his eyes, and he nodded once to confirm he knew the place.

"Make sure it's around there. And make it big."

Lizard pursed his lips into a thin line. "Consider it done. What do I get in return?"

Skelton poked his head out from the doorway and looked up and down the street. He had checked for CCTV as he entered the street. When he was certain the coast was clear, he reached into his jacket pocket and pulled out the package. He thrust it towards Lizard, pressurising him into hiding it quickly. "There's enough weed in there for you to make five hundred quid, and there's another five hundred quid in cash."

Lizard snatched the package and shoved it down the front of his trousers with a smile. His trousers bulged. "Do you like my package?" He laughed, thrusting his hips forward.

Skelton rolled his eyes, and despite his reluctance to touch the man, he grabbed Lizard by his jacket and pulled him into the doorway, slamming him against the wall.

Lizard's face flushed pale with fear, as he gasped for breath.

"You need to understand one thing. I'm the boss. You do as I say. If you keep acting like this, you'll get picked up before you even get to the end of the street. Now I don't know about you, but I don't fancy your chances inside when people find out you've been a copper's snitch. Lags in prison that your careless words have put away."

Skelton let the ominous silence settle between them.

It took a few moments before Lizard nodded.

"I was just kidding, man. Chill out. I'm careful. You know that."

Skelton smiled and released Lizard. "I'm glad you're thinking my way. You see, I can make your life very difficult. But there are other people that you really don't want to get on the wrong end of. People who'd make me look like Paddington Bear at a picnic. And whether or not you believe me, I would like you to live a long and happy life," Skelton sneered.

Lizard pulled back his shoulders, attempting to regain some of his dignity as he straightened his jacket. "Message understood. I'll drop you a text once it's done."

Skelton shook his head. "Don't text or call me. Just do it. I'll hear about it in the morning."

And with that, Skelton checked that the coast was clear before he stepped out the doorway, and made his way back towards the Tube station.

25

JADE REVERSED her car into the only available parking spot at the mortuary. For this time of the afternoon, the mortuary was still busy. Most scheduled post-mortems took place in the morning, allowing the pathologist to complete his reports in the afternoon.

They hovered by the front door, waiting to be buzzed in. Jade shuffled nervously from one foot to the other. There was nothing about a post-mortem that bothered her, they needed to be done. Many were straightforward, but she hated ones involving decomposed bodies. Thankfully, there weren't many of those, but the ones that she had attended had bordered on something from a horror movie. Maggots spewing from body cavities like some apocalyptic nightmare and liquefied brain matter pouring out of openings in the skull.

Wainwright was examining his tray of tools as Karen and Jade came through to the main examination room. He glanced up and greeted both with a smile. "Good afternoon, ladies. The last one of the day, so let's get this wrapped up.

I would say join me for dinner afterwards, but I doubt either of you will have the appetite after we've delved deep into this fine specimen we have in front of us. A sumptuous banquet fit for a bunch of cannibals."

Karen and Jade exchanged a glance of amusement.

"Shall we begin?"

Karen nodded, as Wainwright began his procedure.

They watched for the next ninety minutes as Wainwright skilfully went through his predetermined stages. He went from a visual inspection and commentary of the body, to opening the body and removing everything inside the cavity. He took nail scrapings for completeness.

As Wainwright had suspected, his investigations identified the cause of death as a gunshot wound, the bullet piercing the heart. He retrieved the bullet and placed it in a small metal dish which he passed to his assistant.

Karen turned away a few times as the sound of organs plopping and splashing into metal specimen trays broke the silence.

Karen and Jade gathered towards the top end of the body as Wainwright and his assistant performed neat incisions to expose Macholl's skull. Having cut through and removed the top portion, Wainwright had taken his time to remove the brain in its entirety. He noted for the record that the organ exhibited some small deterioration to the quality of the brain mass. A possible cause, the early indicators for dementia.

Much to Karen's disappointment, Wainwright identified nothing else that would further her case.

Karen sat in Wainwright's office cradling a cup of coffee. She had sent Jade home after Wainwright had offered to drop her off later. Even though she had been to the mortuary many times, she'd rarely ventured as far as Wainwright's office. And just like his approach, she found his office clean and orderly. There were very few personal effects other than a couple of nondescript paintings on the wall to soften the atmosphere. But it still maintained the clinical feel that seemed to be a common theme throughout the building.

Wainwright had opted to join Karen by taking the spare chair beside her rather than sit on the other side of his desk.

"These are for you…" he said, holding out a plate of chocolate digestive biscuits.

Karen smirked. "I didn't think you'd remember. It's almost romantic."

His lips tugged upward. "I stick to my promises."

With the smell of death and disinfectant still clinging to her, her stomach flipped over in protest, but she took a biscuit from the plate to avoid upsetting him. Taking small bites, she stared down at her coffee, reluctant to face Wainwright.

They enjoyed a comfortable silence as they sipped coffee and relaxed. She knew Wainwright was biding his time, and just as she had expected, he put his cup down, and leant forward, resting his elbows on his knees.

"Karen, I'm worried about you. You haven't seemed yourself lately."

"I'm fine." Karen shrugged, reverting to the standard reply she always offered when she didn't want to talk about something.

"You and I both know that's not the case. What you went through would be hard for anyone to process. Death is an unfortunate eventuality that none of us want to witness. And you watched it happen right before your eyes, powerless to stop it."

Karen pulled her arms into her body. "What can I say, shit happens. Two officers lost their lives on my watch. I screwed up, and I'll carry that guilt for the rest of my life." Her jaws clenched tight. She didn't know whether she would cry or scream.

Wainwright maintained his professional boundaries even though he wanted to reach out and place a reassuring hand on her shoulder to comfort and support her.

"Karen, you didn't screw up. I'm sure you or any other officer in that situation couldn't have predicted the outcome."

Karen thumped her thigh with a tight fist. "But I screwed up. I didn't do a proper risk assessment. I could have protected the witness. I could have had armed officers accompany us. I could have requested that the witness produce her statement in court via video link. I could have…"

Wainwright held out a hand, his palm facing her. "*I could have* is a statement from the past. There's nothing you can do to change the past. But you're allowing the past to control your present. It means you haven't moved on. It's affecting your mood, your judgement, and your sanity."

Karen placed her mug on the table and dropped her face into her hands. She drew her fingers across her face as she raised her eyes to meet his. "How can I move on? I've got the blood of those officers on my hands," she fumed, extending her palms out towards him. "People hate me at work. I bet most of them think it should be me lying face down on the pavement… dead. My every move is being watched. And to be honest, I don't even know who the hell is watching me. I go home every night and try to get off my face just to blot out the shit that's swimming around inside it."

Impulsively, Wainwright reached for her hand, cupping it inside both of his. "Listen, you will make yourself ill if you carry on like this. No one is blaming you. You hate failure. And you see this as a failure. But you are a superb officer. And trust me, I've met many in my career. It will pass, and you need to get back to doing what you're good at doing, protecting the public and solving crimes."

Karen wanted to pull her hand away but was reluctant to for fear of offending Wainwright. With his touch, a small part of her cracked open and welcomed the connection.

"Why?" she whispered.

Wainwright looked perplexed as he narrowed his eyes. Uncertain of her question.

Sensing it, Karen continued, "Why are you spending time talking to me? I know we've known each other for a while, professionally of course, and even though you annoy the hell out of me sometimes, we get on. But why?"

Wainwright smiled. "Despite what you might think, I'm not cold or insensitive. Just because I do what I do here," Wainwright nodded back in the direction of the examination room, "it doesn't mean I don't care. Yes, we are friends. And when friends are troubled, they support each other. I guess what I'm trying to say is that when you're feeling out of sorts, I'm always here if you need a friendly face to talk to or a shoulder to lean on."

Karen sighed and pursed her lips into a smile. She pulled her hand away and rubbed the back of one of his hands. "Thank you."

"For what?"

"The chocolate digestive biscuits." She burst out laughing.

Wainwright joined her as he let out a belly laugh. "Go on, bugger off."

Karen placed a finger to her chin and looked up towards the ceiling. "Um, just one problem with that. You promised to give me a lift home."

Wainwright stood and raised his arms above his head to stretch. "Digestive biscuits, and now a lift home. What's next? Doing your ironing and making you breakfast?"

Karen raised a brow as Wainwright's face flushed blood red after he realised the implications of what he'd said. Neither of them said a word after that as Wainwright locked up and followed her out to the car.

26

DURING THE DRIVE home with Wainwright, they had shared jovial banter. They had both discussed their plans for the evening, and Wainwright had surprised Karen by explaining that he attended dance classes several times a week. He didn't confess to being an exquisite, Latin ballroom dancer, but said he enjoyed the social aspect due to the solitary nature of his job.

Karen had turned down his invitation to come along for a laugh. Even though the idea appealed to her, the thought of tripping over someone's feet, and making a complete fool of herself, pulled her back from doing anything adventurous. She had settled for a Marks & Spencer's microwave meal she had picked up from the high street.

JOLTED BACK TO THE PRESENT, she tapped a pen on her desk as her eyes flicked through the latest update from forensics. Her hunch had proved right. The fingerprints lifted from one wine glass and the letters came back as a positive match for Diane Murphy. To further confirm Diane was at the scene, the long brown strand of hair recovered from one of the pillows and bodily fluids recovered from the bedsheets matched her DNA.

Was Diane having an affair with Macholl behind Taylor's back? But that still doesn't explain why she would gun him down in cold blood.

Despite her racing thoughts, she would have to wait for the ballistics report on the bullet recovered from Macholl. But ballistics had confirmed that the firearm used on Taylor had been used previously, including a firearms incident at a fried chicken shop some months back. At the time it was suspected that the firearm was discharged during a feud between rival gangs.

The suspicion grew as the same gang was targeted again just a week later, and a seventeen-year-old youth died from gunshot wounds. The killing had sparked a postcode war as rival gangs fought running street battles with machetes and zombie knives.

A shiver of surprise moved through her as she considered the latest evidence. Ballistics confirmed that the ammunition and markings on the bullet were linked to the Whitechapel unsolved case that Jade had highlighted from a few years back.

Someone's been concealing this firearm for a few years.

The thought crossed Karen's mind that perhaps rival gangs were competing for the drugs trade, and they were sending out a very clear message when they took out Taylor. That still didn't explain Macholl's murder.

This has to go back further than that.

"Morning, boss," Jade said as she poked her head around the door and stepped into Karen's office holding two mugs of coffee. The aroma quickly filled the room as Jade placed one mug down for Karen.

"Awe bless. Thanks, Jade. I'm in desperate need of my caffeine hit. I've got far too much to do, and not enough time. I've got several twenty-one-day review alerts that have popped up on my screen this morning, and I honestly haven't got a whole day to sit and go through them. Anything new to report?"

"I'm not sure, boss. I've only just got in myself. While my computer was warming up, I made us both a cuppa. Flippin' typical, I wanted to get in early but got stuck talking to Chrissie in the car park. She was just coming off a night shift. Apparently, it was full on last night, and uniform had a nightmare."

Karen gave Jade a questioning look.

Jade's continued, "Yes, shots were fired at the window of an off-licence in Hackney Road. Then a car was set alight about a mile away, which from eyewitness reports suggest it was the same vehicle involved in the firearms incident. And then near to there, residents reported hearing gunfire. So, you can imagine our response. We had ARVs flooding the area, carriers full of TSG, and NPAS providing aerial support."

"Busy night then. Any arrests?"

Jade shook her head as she took another sip from her coffee. "Wild goose chase, I think. I'll give you an update on the cases when I've logged on," she said, standing up and strolling out.

The use of firearms was an ever-increasing threat and added a new dimension to many of the cases that MIT dealt with. Gang members could pick up handguns for just a few hundred pounds. She had heard that some underworld armourers were loaning out weapons for shootings at two hundred and fifty pounds for a non-fatal wounding and five hundred pounds for an assassination.

It horrified her that firearms were loaned out in the same way that you would rent a movie online, or a book from the library, only returning it once the crime had been completed. That made it even harder for the police to track down the firearms.

The phrase "needle in a haystack" sprung to mind as Karen ran a hand through her hair, and headed for the video room.

Now that Karen could place Diane at Macholl's apartment, it was a fair assumption that Diane may have been the last person to see Macholl alive. She grabbed the nearest terminal, and punched in the details for Columbia Road pulling up all the intelligence and video footage gathered so far. They had retrieved further footage from the off-licence and the pub close by. Karen hoped they would be able to identify Diane's car either travelling to or from Macholl's apartment during the night.

Knowing that a resident had placed the call to the emergency services at two seventeen a.m., Karen checked the tapes from eleven p.m. through to three a.m. She was looking for a Mercedes or one of the two BMWs she had seen parked outside Taylor's residence when they had first attended. It was a long shot, but if she could identify Diane in the vicinity at the time that the shots were reported, it would give her a reason to bring the woman in.

Karen squinted as she studied the footage. She had set the speed at twice the normal rate, so everything she saw on screen was moving faster than normal, allowing her to go through the footage quicker. She jolted as a door behind opened.

"Karen, I've been looking for you. How's the case progressing?" Skelton asked.

Skelton hovered just a few inches over her shoulder, his presence unnerving Karen. She could smell the faint whiff of tobacco wafting in her direction. He seemed to disregard etiquette and common decency as he inched closer, his thigh brushing against her arm. Karen shifted in her seat, leaning her body away from him.

"We are making good inroads, sir. Diane Murphy is a person of interest to us in Macholl's case. Forensics have confirmed her presence in the hours leading up to his death. I'm just scanning through CCTV footage to see if I can place her at the scene," she replied, pointing towards a monitor.

Skelton crossed his arms. "Is she a suspect for Taylor's murder?"

"Not yet, sir. But she's still a person of interest."

Skelton cleared his throat. "The HOLMES2 activity log says you're still doing searches on the Connells. How does that link into our current case?"

"I'm not sure yet, sir. It's just a line of enquiry. I've got to make sure I cover every single avenue. I can't afford any fuck ups. There was a firearms incident some time back in Whitechapel. The shooter was never identified, but the victim was possibly linked to the Connells. Because it was on our patch, and it was a firearms incident, I'm just checking for any links, especially now that ballistics confirmed that it was the same firearm used in the Whitechapel murder."

Skelton shook his head. "You're wasting your time, Karen. I think you're looking in the wrong direction. It's like you've got a chip on your shoulder about the Connells. In all honesty, they are way too big for this. If it was anything to do with them, I'm certain they would have covered their tracks. They are more slippery than an eel in a bush tucker trial."

"Yes, sir, but…"

"There's no but there, Karen. Stop wasting your time. It's an unhealthy obsession. We need results. And we need them quickly. If you need leads, go to the Copthorne. There's plenty of snivelling little shits there."

She watched his reflection as he turned and headed out of the door. Her gaze fixed on the closed door a few moments. Her mind was telling her one thing, her heart was telling her something else.

27

"UNHEALTHY OBSESSION... MY ARSE." Skelton's flippant words returned to her, and Karen fumed. Every time she tried to make progress, her boss appeared to sink her plans. "There's no unhealthy obsession about it. I'm following leads and links, even if they're bloody tenuous," she muttered.

There were multiple OCGs in and around Shoreditch. Many were small-time. But most of the crime could be attributed to just a few key players. There were "the Roubles", a Russian criminal organisation. They specialised in fraud, counterfeiting, and high-tech crime. Most of their revenue was ghosted back to their connections in Russia.

And then there were the Connells. A major criminal organisation run by Sally Connell. She had taken over after her father was gunned down outside a pub in Hackney by a rival firm. Her brothers, Terry and Steve ably assisted her. Since the late 1960s, the Connells were heavily involved in armed robbery, contract killing, drugs trafficking and other racketeering-related activities within London's underworld. Following the downfall of the Kray brothers, the Connells were one of several criminal organisations who had filled the vacuum within the London underworld.

There followed a highly publicised gangland war during the 1990s as rival families fought for control. The Connells succeeded; they were ruthless and unforgiving. Media reports had linked the family to around twenty-five murders. But their organisation was so complex, that very few of their members had been brought to justice, thanks in part to bent coppers and lawyers on their payroll.

Karen knew the Connells were connected directly or indirectly to every major crime that had been committed in the area for the past few years. To her, this was both personal and professional.

She carried on scanning the video footage of Columbia Road, pausing the tape every time a car came into view. Footage had been retrieved from three different locations, the off-licence, the pub, and a small boutique shop. The team had worked tirelessly to combine the footage so she could watch all three feeds at the same time on one screen, but the dark, grainy footage proved challenging. The street lights provided little in terms of illumination to help her.

Karen froze the tape again when the figure of a person walked past the pub. She zoomed in, but the closer she focused on the person, the more pixelated it became. Her mind spun as she analysed the image. She switched to the feed from the off-licence and estimated that the figure would have walked past the off-licence just a few minutes earlier. The feed was far clearer because of the bright glare of the shop lighting up the pavement.

"Gotcha."

Karen zoomed in on the image again and took a screenshot. She saw the distinctive outline and features of Diane Murphy. Karen shook her head. No wonder she hadn't seen Diane's car, she had come on foot. Diane had probably parked some distance away. Karen checked the time frame, the timestamp showed eleven thirty-seven p.m. And she was walking towards Macholl's apartment.

Her eyes were sore, her shoulders stiff, and her back ached from sitting in one position. Staring at CCTV footage was one of the less glamorous activities required for the job. Thankfully, she had a small time frame to work on. But she had been on other jobs where officers had trawled through days and sometimes weeks of footage. Twelve-hour shifts, day after day, staring at a monitor looking for that one clue, or piece of evidence that would give them the breakthrough in a case.

She paused again when she saw Diane's figure passing the pub and coming into view of the off-licence camera. Karen paused the tape again and checked the time. The timestamp confirmed that she was walking away from Macholl's apartment at one forty-three a.m.

"Bollocks." Diane had left his apartment at least thirty minutes before the emergency services received the first calls. Karen continued to study the footage until two twenty-one a.m. when she saw the first area cars and armed response units arriving.

Karen was confident that Diane hadn't been directly involved in the murder of Macholl. She had left the scene at least thirty minutes before, and unless there was another way to access Macholl's apartment, she hadn't returned.

KAREN UPDATED Jade as they made their way over to Taylor's place. Despite what she had observed in the footage, Karen still felt the need to question Diane's movements. There was still a chance that Diane may have spotted something unusual as she left the apartment. There was also a burning question in the back of Karen's mind. Diane's son. She had seen Ben with Macholl less than two days ago.

Once there, it took a few moments before Diane opened the door. She looked tired and weary, her eyes darting between both officers. A look of despondency etched with annoyance was all she could offer.

"Why can't you leave me alone? If you come around here any more, you might as well move in!" she boomed, her voice echoing in the hallway behind her.

Karen and Jade followed her, not waiting to be invited.

"We've got a few more questions we need to ask you."

"Questions, questions. That's all you bloody do. You should be out there catching the scum," she uttered as she walked to the lounge, not looking to see if they were following.

Karen and Jade stood as Diane slumped into one sofa and tilted her head back on the cushions. Jade walked over towards the window and perched herself against the windowsill, taking out her pen and notepad. It was a warm morning, and she enjoyed the warmth of the sun on her back. The golden arching rays crept around her, creating an angelic halo that framed her shape in the window.

"When was the last time you saw Dean Macholl?"

Diane shook her head. "I don't know. The party?"

Karen offered the smallest of smiles. Diane was a lousy liar. "Diane, Dean Macholl was murdered in the early hours of yesterday morning. He was shot dead in his flat."

Diane's eyes widened in surprise and grief. Her bottom lip trembled, and her jaw shivered as she wrapped her arms around her chest. Karen noticed the woman's eyes misting over.

"Dead?"

"Yup." Karen's answer was deliberately blunt. "What were you doing at Dean Macholl's apartment?"

The question took Diane by surprise, her eyes flickering in panic. She tightened her lips into a grimace. The reaction didn't go unnoticed by Karen and Jade.

"I wasn't there."

"Oh, really. So the person we saw in CCTV footage at eleven thirty-seven walking in the direction of Macholl's apartment, and then leaving again at one forty-three a.m. precisely, wasn't you?"

"Why does that matter?"

"Why? Because I don't think you've been completely truthful with us. They found your DNA in his bed. How long have you been carrying on with him?"

Diane's face flushed blood red as she clenched her hands into a tight ball. Her lips mouthed words silently as she fought to gain clarity. "It was just a one-off. I got a bit tipsy, and one thing led to another."

"Don't bullshit me, Diane. You were probably the last person to see him alive. You don't just turn up at someone's apartment, have a couple of glasses of wine, and jump into the sack with someone you've hardly seen."

For a moment, her own thoughts stunned Karen. She had done exactly that the night she had met Neil in a bar.

"We discovered letters addressed to Dean, and signed by the initial D. We've had forensics examine the letters, and your prints were on them."

"I… I…"

As much as Diane tried to hold it in, the pain came out like a roar from her throat in the form of a silent scream. The bead of tears fell one after another without a sign of stopping, muffled sobs racking against her chest.

Karen and Jade exchanged a glance. Karen looked towards the box of tissues on a small table towards the far end of the room, and guided Jade with her eyes towards it. Jade cottoned on and went to retrieve it before offering them to Diane. Diane pulled out a few and wiped her face and blew her nose.

"I think there's more that you need to tell us, Diane, don't you?" Karen's voice softened slightly, but she wasn't letting Diane off the hook so easily.

28

DIANE LOOKED A SHADOW OF HERSELF. The aggression and bluntness she had displayed on their previous visits had melted away. She looked frail now, uncertain and scared. She considered herself a strong woman. She'd had to be for the sake of her son. As a family, they mixed in the most violent circles of the criminal underworld. Any sign of weakness was a sign of vulnerability, and Jack hadn't wanted that.

She stared down at the sodden tissues in her hands. Lost in her thoughts, she tore long strips off and scrunched them into tiny balls.

"Diane?"

Diane didn't hear Karen calling her. It was as if she had blocked out the world around her.

"Diane. We need to hear your side of the story. We've got a double murder on our hands. And both men were part of your life."

The woman looked up and met Karen's steady gaze. There was an emptiness in her bloodshot eyes. Her lids were sore and red, her lips moistened with tears. She nodded her head a few times.

"Dean and I were an item many years ago. We were in love," she said nostalgically, her eyes trailing off towards a space in the room. "Dean and Jack were associates back then. Dean introduced me to Jack."

The penny dropped for Karen and she knew where the confession was headed before Diane even continued.

"There was something about Jack. I couldn't put my finger on it. They were both wrong'uns. Dean was a charmer, and Jack, well Jack was macho, loud and aggressive. He was never short of female attention. He always had a different woman on his arm. It was like bees to a honeypot. You can imagine how I felt when he gave me the eye."

"So you saw Jack behind Dean's back?"

The woman nodded once and bit her bottom lip, a mixture of shame and embarrassment forcing her to pull her arms in closer to her sides.

"The problem was while I was seeing him, he already had another woman. And he wasn't prepared to let her go. She worked in a bookies, and he wanted to rob it. That was his speciality, armed robbery, hitting easy targets like bookies, off-licences, and that type of thing. And of course, this woman was prepared to do anything to help him."

"Is this the last bookies they raided before they went their separate ways?"

"Yeah. It all went wrong. He told me that he needed her, and once he was done with the raid he would give her the boot. But on the night, there were two members of staff working behind the counter. This woman and her manager. Anyway, the manager decided to have a go. It got out of hand, and Jack pulled the trigger. It missed the bloke but hit the woman. She died."

"So Dean didn't pull the trigger?"

"No." She shook her head. "Dean didn't. Jack did. But Jack wasn't gonna take the fall for it, so he spread the word that Dean did it. Before you knew it, there were loads of snouts out there willing to claim that Dean was behind the raid, and that he shot the woman."

Karen remained silent, letting Diane carry on with her recollections. Diane paused for a moment, doubt deep in thought.

"Dean had no choice. He was gonna be set up for a murder he didn't commit or get lynched. He had to go on the run."

Karen regarded her. "You could have said something to protect an innocent man?"

Diane shook her head as her eyes widened. "No. No. You just don't do things like that to Jack. I would have been as good as dead, if I opened my mouth. Jack had warned me a few times that I would have to keep that secret until the day I died. But it would be my choice when I died, if you know what I mean?"

Karen nodded. There was something else on her mind she needed Diane to explain.

"After Ben left the station, I saw him cross the road to be met by Dean. How did he know Dean? Was Dean trying to intimidate Ben? Was Ben trying to protect you?" The avalanche of questions seemed to trip on Karen's tongue.

“No. It was not like that.”

Karen crossed her arms. “Well, what was it like then? You are one of the last people to see Macholl alive. Ben had the perfect reason to murder Jack and Macholl… to protect you from any further hurt.”

An uncomfortable silence settled over the room as Diane processed her thoughts. She tried to make some sense of the events that had shattered her life in the last few days.

As Diane contemplated, Jade’s patience was wearing thin. She shifted uncomfortably on the windowsill, the edge of the wood making her backside numb. She cleared her throat gently to attract Karen’s attention. Karen looked over her shoulder as Jade willed Karen to push on with her eyes.

“Diane?”

Diane dropped her gaze to the floor as her shoulders dropped. “Jack hated Ben. He never wanted anything to do with him. All Jack wanted to do was kick him out, and I had to plead with him on a weekly basis to let Ben stay. He never showed Ben one ounce of love or compassion. It was as if Ben never existed in Jack’s eyes.”

“Why?” Karen probed.

“Ben is Dean’s son.”

29

Karen leant back in her chair and tipped it back and forth. Macholl being Ben's father put a different perspective on her case. Ben had a motive for killing Taylor, but she questioned whether he would have had a motive to kill his own father. *Is there more to this than I've uncovered?*

Following Skelton's "suggestion" she had instructed the team to gather as much CCTV footage as they could of the Copthorne estate on the date of Taylor's murder. From her past dealings, she knew the estate had featured heavily in Taylor's empire. It had proved a useful conduit for the supply and distribution of drugs. And it was quite possible that either Taylor had upset one of the distributors, or someone on the estate had decided they wanted a bigger slice of the cake. Intelligence on the HOLMES2 system confirmed that there were several smaller pockets of criminality, but most of the illegal activity was attributed to Darren Finch, aged thirty-two, a drug dealer with connections to Taylor and the Connells.

She could visualise the hierarchical chain with the Connells on top, followed by the likes of Taylor, with street rats like Finch and his runners languishing at the bottom. Each part of the chain chomping at the bit to find a way to move up the ladder.

Karen's phone chimed, and she stared at the screen for several moments. She had cancelled the reminder a few times in recent days. Each time the guilt haunted her. After all this time it still cut just as deep. She had to remind herself that while she couldn't undo her misdeeds, she'd dedicated her life to making a difference in the world.

Maybe that was her way of avoiding emotions she kept tightly locked away. It seemed unfair that no matter how much she strived to be the woman her conscience wanted her to be, it taunted her with her failures. Each time the regrets emerged, she would diligently analyse them again, hoping that this time her mind would be satisfied with her self-professed remorse.

Karen scrolled through her contacts until she found and dialled the number for Broomfield Residential Care Home. After reaching the reception, they put her through to her contact, Nurse Robyn Allen.

"Karen. It's lovely to hear from you. It's been a long time, and we were hoping to have heard from you sooner, or at least a visit."

Nurse Allen's words cut through her like the pointed tip of a shard of glass. She glanced up towards the ceiling unsure how to reply, knowing anything she said would sound like a feeble excuse.

"I'm sorry, Robyn. I've meant to call for a few days but been tied up with a major case." She felt pangs of guilt for just saying those words.

"I know. And I know you're busy. But Jane looks forward to your visits. She is less irritable, and so much calmer after you've gone."

Robyn's words stifled Karen's breath. She could feel her eyes moistening. There was nothing she could say or do that would make the situation any better. She felt helpless, selfish and a poor excuse for a sister.

"How is she?" Karen asked.

"You know… She has good days and bad days. The physiotherapist visits her every day and does her best to make sure that Jane's mobility doesn't worsen. Her feeding is just the same. We get the occasional murmur and semi-constructed word slip from her lips. But other than that, nothing has changed."

It was nothing she'd hadn't heard before. Her sister's condition had remained the same for as long as she could remember. "I will try my hardest to get there in the next few days. I would like to see her."

"And I'm sure she would *love* to see you," the nurse said.

With the lift in Robyn's tone, Karen imagined that the woman was smiling as she said those words. The phone calls were always awkward. She never knew what to say, and they would cover the same ground each time. Karen would ask how her sister was, if she was being fed well, and whether there were any further complications or issues she needed to know about. Robyn, in return, would update her on her sister's condition, and would always find a way of asking when Karen could spare the time to visit.

Karen hung up after promising to call back to arrange a time. She stared at the phone as she placed it back on the desk.

Following difficulties conceiving, and after her mother, Anne, had suffered a miscarriage during her second pregnancy, her parents had been blessed with Jane. Her sister was born prematurely with a compressed umbilical cord which led to a situation called birth asphyxia and brain damage. Jane had lived in a care home for most of her life, suffering with seizures, blindness and an undeveloped brain. Motor disorders, development delays, and behavioural disturbances were some of the complications that the nursing team had to deal with while they provided her with twenty-four-hour care. Jane was thirty-six years old but had a mental age of a twelve-year-old. Karen had promised to pop in once a week, but only managed once a month.

She looked around her office and wondered what life was all about. She had a younger sister who had never experienced life, and come to think of it, neither had she. She was married to the job, and if she was honest with herself, used it as a distraction. She would much rather be buried under piles of paperwork, than sit at home and process her thoughts, emotions and her vulnerability. If she took a moment to do that, she feared what she might find, and whether she could handle it.

After the events eight months ago, she had been advised to seek help rather than bottle up her emotions. But she'd never plucked up the courage to follow it through, despite agreeing to it. She'd shuddered at the thought of exposing her darkest thoughts and releasing feelings and emotions entombed inside her mind. What if she freaked out, broke down, or sobbed uncontrollably while working her way through a box of tissues? Would she be any better? Or would they say she was so broken that she would have to resign?

Each outcome terrified her.

Karen felt the panic begin like a cluster of spark plugs in her abdomen. Tension grew in her face and limbs as her mind replayed the ambush. Her pupils stayed fixed wide with fear as she glanced around the room, while clutching the edge of the desk. The thoughts galloped inside her head. She wanted them to slow so she could breathe but they wouldn't. Breaths came in gasps and she felt like blacking out. Her heart hammered inside her chest. The room spun out of control.

"Shit."

She dropped her head on the desk, trying to make everything slow to something her brain and body could cope with. Nausea rolled over her in waves.

"Breathe… breathe… breathe…" She begged herself.

A cold shiver ran through her as she pulled herself back into the room.

"Jesus, not again…"

30

KAREN KEPT her head down as she darted towards the ladies' toilets. She pushed through the door with such force it slammed against the wall behind, the noise startling her. She glanced at the long line of cubicles. They were empty, *thank God.* She half bent over a sink and turned on the cold tap. Forming a makeshift cup with her hands, Karen allowed them to fill before splashing the water across her face. The cold chill met with her burning hot cheeks, turning the water lukewarm. She splashed more water, doing it repeatedly, hoping it would calm her. It felt soothing, relaxing, so much so that she wanted to fill the sink and dive head first in to it.

She laid her hands on the edge of the sink and looked up to see her damp face in the mirror. The edges of her hair stuck together in wet clumps. *God, I look like shit.* "Pull yourself together, stay calm, and lots of deep breaths. It will be okay. It will be okay. It will… be… okay."

She pulled in a large lungful of air while gripping the side of the bowl, her fingernails turning white as they pressed into the enamel. Karen cleared her throat before stepping away and grabbing a handful of paper towels to wipe her face.

"You can do this," she assured herself before she turned and left.

Karen made her way along the corridor and slipped back into her office without anyone noticing. A sigh of relief escaped her lips as she dropped into her chair and glanced through the glass walls of her office to see if anyone was watching her. Convinced that she'd got away with it, she did her best to put it to one side as her shaky hand grabbed the mouse and opened the video files again.

Her mind was a melting pot of confusion and thoughts. Karen tried her hardest to push them to one side as she flicked through the video footage. The images she saw could have come from any council estate the length and breadth of the country. Elderly people shuffled in and out of the apartment blocks. A parent pushed their small child in a swing, and the unemployed youths played pranks on each other and intimidated the residents. But she cast them from her mind without a second thought, because Darren Finch's visage consumed her focus. She checked the timestamp. It was a little after eleven thirty in the morning, and she doubted if Finch would be awake. She put the tape on fast forward.

Karen's eyes grew heavier from the intense concentration. *This really has to be one of the most mind-numbing chores that any officer can go through.*

On the verge of nodding off at her desk, she spotted something which had her reaching for the mouse and clicking pause. She took the tape back a few seconds, and pressed play again at normal speed as she watched a group of seven youths appear from behind one of the apartment blocks on the estate. They strutted and bowled as they made their way towards the centre square. Each one wore a black hoodie or jacket with its hood raised in order to obscure much of their face. A token black scarf shielded the lower half, just leaving them with menacing stares.

Karen sat up and studied the images. None of them appeared to be Finch. She thought they looked in their late teens and early twenties. Her suspicions were confirmed when another figure appeared a few yards behind. This one didn't try to hide his face. *Got you, Finch.* He walked just as slow, his swagger suggesting ownership of his patch. He joined the others by some railings that skirted the playground.

She watched for the next few minutes as the men slouched against the railings, smoking and staring around the estate. She was just about to speed through the tape when she noticed a change in their behaviour. There were sharp and jagged movements as they glanced around in all directions and exchanged words. The brashness and confidence they had displayed just a few minutes earlier faded as they huddled together looking in one direction.

Something from just off camera had alarmed them. It took a few moments before three men appeared. They had the same swagger and confidence, except these men were older, considerably older, and leading the trio was Jack Taylor. Karen assumed that the two men behind him, who had spread out into an arc, were his backup.

The group of youths backed away, leaving Finch isolated. Karen watched as Taylor strode towards Finch, leaving the two heavies a few yards behind. Finch and Taylor stood nose to nose with Taylor jabbing his finger into Finch's chest. Remarkably, Finch held his ground as Taylor appeared to unleash a volley of words. The youths loitered in the background, remaining still. Even though they outnumbered the men, Karen knew they would be no match for the walking muscleheads with Taylor.

The altercation soon turned to violence as Taylor launched a missile of a punch which sent Finch tumbling to the ground. Before Finch could gather himself, Taylor jumped him, unleashing a flurry of punches. Having battered Finch, Taylor stood and dusted off his hands before turning and calmly walking away. Once Taylor disappeared from the image, Karen watched as the youths edged their way back towards Finch, crowding around him.

Karen stared at the footage as a new suspect in Taylor's murder emerged right before her eyes.

31

Witnessing the nasty fight fuelled Karen's curiosity further. She had paused the tape and gone to the kitchen to make herself a strong cup of coffee. Since she had hours of video footage to trawl through, being stuck in a hot, stuffy room made her feel sleepy.

Karen made her way back and settled in her seat again. She blew out her cheeks as she clicked the mouse and set the tape in fast forward again. Cars came and went. The occasional delivery van crawled around the different apartment blocks looking for the right address. Even delivery drivers questioned their safety, or more precisely, the safety of their load. She watched each driver race around to the back of their van, retrieve the package that needed to be delivered, and race off to the address, before returning just a minute later.

Boring, boring, dull.

She stared at the screen, her mind drifting to thoughts of going home this evening and curling up on the sofa with

Manky and a large glass of white wine. Due to her erratic hours, she often recorded episodes of her favourite TV series. Any crime drama or psychological thriller interested her, but she binge-watched *Ozark*, *Luther*, and *Sons of Anarchy*. If she wanted to switch off and just have a laugh, she would revert to old episodes of *Only Fools and Horses*, *The Vicar of Dibley* and *The Office*.

Karen spent the next few hours scouring through the tapes, searching for anything connected to her case. At times, the footage looked like a comedy film as people scurried around while she had it in fast-forward review. There were moments where the estate appeared empty with no movement at all. She took a few more breaks to rest her eyes, asking Jade to step in and continue to monitor the tapes as she popped out to get some fresh air.

JUNE WAS ALWAYS a good time of year. Recently, May and June had offered more of what she would consider summer weather with brilliant sunshine and warm days. They contrasted with July and August, often far more temperamental and unseasonal months.

Karen felt a sense of frustration. The streets were busy with shopworkers and office staff, the roads were packed with black cabs, red buses, couriers on motorcycles, and delivery vans that clogged up and slowed down the traffic. The sounds of London life echoed around her, and the air smelt of pollution and grime. On a bright, sunny day like this she wished she was in Frinton with its wide, sandy beach, and small scattering of shops and cafés. Frinton-on-Sea represented her childhood, and she had spent many a weekend with her aunts and uncles. She'd rarely been there with her mum and dad. Sadly, they were too busy looking after her sister Jane, but not wanting her to miss out, her parents had made sure that she enjoyed some downtime away from their hectic and challenging home life.

A buzz from her phone jolted Karen from her reverie as a text from Jade revealed she'd found something interesting.

"What have you got, Jade?" Karen asked as she stepped back into her room. She pulled up a chair alongside Jade.

"Well, I've carried on looking through the tape, and there was nothing that caught my attention."

Karen's heart sank on hearing those words. Everything had to be a royal pain in her arse when it came to this case.

"But when I got to two thirty a.m. I noticed something of interest."

They both stared at a frozen image of the estate, now shrouded in darkness, the only illumination from a handful of street lights that surrounded the playground and the illuminated walkways in each block.

Jade hit play, and the tape continued rolling at normal speed. They watched as one by one a group of figures appeared between two blocks of apartments. At first they couldn't make out their gender, but as they gathered closer to the playground, the street lights illuminated the shadows. There were five figures, all male, and from what Karen could see, dressed in similar clothes to what she had seen earlier. Jade zoomed in, and Karen noticed a white emblem on the back of one of the youths' jacket. It looked like the outline of a fist, the same image from the earlier footage.

Karen pointed out that at least two of the youths appeared to be carrying long objects which from a distance were hard to identify. They could have been small scaffold poles, or lumps of wood, or even crowbars. Regardless, they were carrying offensive weapons. She saw no signs of a firearm, but that didn't mean that one of them hadn't concealed a gun.

They both watched as the group jostled with each other in a display of mock aggression. From the edge of the footage, another figure appeared and joined them. They gathered together in a small circle as if discussing something. Whatever they were talking about only lasted a few minutes before they moved off as a group and disappeared out of shot. Jade zoomed in again as the group left, and Karen saw the distinctive outline of Finch. He was taller and broader than the rest.

"Anything else?"

Jade nodded as she pressed the fast forward. "I continued rolling the tape until six a.m., and the same group came back at five forty-three a.m."

Karen watched as Jade replayed that section of tape. This time the group's movements were quicker. They congregated close to the playground, talking in a huddled circle before splitting up and heading in different directions. She noticed Finch glancing around before he jogged back to one of the apartment blocks. Karen focused on his left hand that appeared to be pressed against the left side of his jacket.

Does he have a gun concealed?

32

KAREN CAUGHT Skelton coming out of a senior management meeting. He looked bored, dishevelled and grisly, but he looked like that most of the time. His hair was ruffled, his tie hung loosely, and the top button of his shirt was undone.

"Sir, have you got a moment?"

He drew his lips into a thin line, staring at her for a few moments.

Karen felt her skin crawl as his eyes burrowed into hers. He was the only man who made her feel that way. He was lecherous, conniving, arrogant and rude. Skelton was the epitome of everything she strived not to be. He flicked his head towards an empty office, and Karen followed him.

After closing the door behind them, Skelton dropped his notebook on the table, and crossed his arms waiting for Karen to speak first.

Karen filled him in on the information she'd discovered from the footage of the estate, and the need to bring Finch in for questioning.

"Just because Taylor gave him a kicking it doesn't mean he went seeking revenge."

"I get that, sir, but it offers a plausible reason? Revenge? And we know that Finch and his gang have used firearms in the past."

Skelton paced around the room before stopping by the window as he considered her reasons for a while.

"So you want to go in there, kicking down doors and stirring up more anti-police feelings?"

"I don't see it that way. Finch and his associates make lives miserable on that estate. We'd be doing the residents a favour. We can go in softly."

"Not if firearms are involved! If you're going in there, you go in with armed backup."

"Understood. So do I have your consent?"

Skelton grimaced. "Go for it. Clearing out scum like that won't be a bad thing. Get a warrant and firearms sorted, and then go in. And Karen, get it right. The *safety* of our officers comes first. Make sure you do a thorough risk assessment."

With those clipped words, Skelton left, seemingly in a rush to get on. Karen sighed. She should have been excited, but Skelton had a knack of knocking the wind out of her with a few chosen words.

Karen made her way back and pushed through the double doors. "Okay, team. Gather around as we've got a potential lead to follow up."

The team surfaced from their workstations and perched on the desks surrounding the incident board. Karen stood to one side and looked at the various images pinned to it. The faces of Taylor, Macholl, Diane Murphy and her son Ben stared back at the team. Karen had drawn red lines with arrows going back and forth between them to mark their connections. Photographs from both crime scenes had been added along with close-ups of both bullets retrieved from the victims. Karen waited for the remaining support staff and other detectives to join them from the back of the room. She now had the full attention of over twenty officers. She cleared her throat to quiet the myriad of hushed conversations that rippled through the crowd.

Karen began by explaining how she and Jade had reviewed CCTV footage of the Copthorne estate, and how they had witnessed a serious altercation between Darren Finch and Jack Taylor just hours before Taylor's murder. She went on to explain how Finch and his gang had met less than an hour prior to when Taylor had been murdered, continuing to add that the very same group returned shortly after that two-hour window.

"We know from past intelligence that Finch and his gang have used violence and firearms, and it's highly likely that Finch may still be in possession of a firearm. We need to bring Finch in for questioning in relation to the assault and see if he can shed any light on why Taylor may have been murdered."

Brad waved his pen in the air. "Boss, can we assume that Finch may have had wanted revenge for being attacked by Taylor?"

Karen nodded. "We can't be certain, but it's plausible. And I think it's worth giving Finch a tug to see what the scrote has to say."

"Any news on the ballistics from the bullet recovered from Macholl?"

"Not yet, Steve. But it would be great if you could chase up for me, since ballistics have had it for nearly twenty-four hours already."

"So what's our next step?" asked an officer.

"We will execute a search warrant this evening. It could turn volatile, and there's a possibility we may find firearms on the premises which is why I've arranged for NPAS, and SCO19."

A wave of murmurs rippled amongst the group as officers exchanged looks, and a few eyebrows raised in a mixture of surprise and excitement.

"When are we going in?" another officer asked.

"As soon as we've got the resources in place. A search warrant is being prepared at the moment, and as soon as this briefing ends, I'll be organising all the extra resources and then we'll go, so don't make any plans to leave for the time being."

Karen made her way back to the office as soon as the briefing ended, a busy night ahead of her. First she organised the team she needed for this evening. She couldn't afford to mess up, so made sure she picked the right people for the job.

With a few moments to spare while she waited for confirmation on the search warrant, Karen looked over the top of her computer screen to make sure that the coast was clear before she logged in to one of the many databases that they had access to. Ever-present was her need to go over case files and intelligence dating back eight months and beyond. The ambush was never far from her mind, and while she got on with the *day* job, she spent some of her time trying to find the missing pieces that would allow her to put that difficult period in her career to rest.

There was a someone she was looking for, but strangely wasn't sure exactly who it was, only that the intelligence held on the HOLMES2 system could help her find it. She checked out Finch's connections and drew a blank. She did the same with Taylor and again hit a dead end. She moved on to looking at the connections and intelligence gathered on the Connells. The information they had on the system was sketchy. The Connells were far too clever to leave much of a footprint. But if anyone had access to firearms and the muscle to pull this off, it was the Connells. It was widely known in police circles that the Connells distributed guns through their network and connections.

After Karen flipped back and forth from one record to another, a half an hour of searching gave her the name she needed. She scribbled it down along with an address before slipping the note into her back pocket.

Karen had one last call to make. She felt a pang of guilt race through her as she got through. Following a short conversation, Karen confirmed that she would be along later that evening although she couldn't confirm the time as she was in the middle of an operation.

NIGHT-TIME TWISTED BACK AROUND AGAIN. Children were tucked in, and the homeless walked the streets looking for food and doorways to sleep in. Darkness brought the primal nature to the fore, a heady trance for those men who craved dominance and power. They stalked amongst the thrill seekers, the partygoers, their faces set to an underscored snarl. After sunset each person morphed into either a player or a nobody.

Skelton didn't want to be a nobody. The streets were his. He had spent most of his life around here and knew the area like the back of his hand. He knew where the druggies went to score, and where the working girls took their punters for a quick blow job or a fuck and he knew where there was no CCTV.

Skelton waited in an alleyway, checking his watch. He didn't need to emerge from the shadows because they knew where to find him. He dragged hard on his cigarette, enjoying the buzz as nicotine flooded his system. The smoke drifted out of his mouth and up towards his eyes, the familiar sting making his eyes water. Despite telling Karen to stop snooping for dirt on the Connells, the HOLMES2 system reports confirmed multiple searches and cross-checks on the Connells and their associates. Karen had trawled intelligence reports, looked at the profiles of anyone with links to the Connells, and had put in requests with the NCA for further information.

He couldn't afford to have a loose cannon interfering in his business. She was getting too close. If she picked up anything, she wouldn't let go.

Yes she's a liability and sooner or later I won't have any choice but to make sure she no longer poses a threat.

He heard the loud purring of an engine as a vehicle cruised up the street. It turned right into the alleyway and pulled up alongside him. The blacked-out rear window of the slick, black Range Rover slid down. Sally Connell's face appeared from behind, her bleach-blonde short bobbed hair stood out in the darkened cabin. Her sharp features and high cheekbones added a coldness to her face.

"Well done the other night. The distractions helped. You've been a good boy. I've got work to take care of now, but drop by in an hour and I'll give you something which I'm sure you'll enjoy."

Like a little puppy that had been praised for not shitting on the carpet, Skelton felt pleased with himself. He afforded himself a smile as his breath quickened and his groin ached at the prospect of having Sally again.

"So what did you want?" she asked, waving her phone in reference to his text message.

"Heath is organising a raid over at the Copthorne this evening. I wanted to warn you so that none of your outfit were in the area dropping off *goods*."

Sally remained silent for a few moments as she pursed her lips, not averting her gaze from Skelton. "Who is she after?"

"That toerag Finch. She thinks he may have been involved in the Taylor murder, so she's going in heavy. Heath has intel on the ground confirming that Finch is holed up there at his girlfriend's place. Just be careful."

Sally said nothing as her face disappeared behind the black window. The Range Rover rumbled down the alleyway before turning left and disappearing into the next street along.

Skelton pulled up the collar on his jacket. He had just enough time to go home to grab a shower and pop a blue pill.

33

Waking up was no longer the pleasure it was as a child. There was a fleeting moment when she felt whole again but it evaporated faster than summer rain off the dry, hot earth. Eyelids that were drooping and leaden with sleep snapped open as violently as if the wailing sirens had woken her. Molly squeezed her soft, lumpy pillow as she let the tears roll down her cheeks.

With nothing to do during the afternoon, Molly had gone to bed and slept for a few hours.

Waking up could be harsh, especially if her dreams were better than her reality, and most of the time they were. The saddest part was that the memory of her dreams faded – even if she was lucky enough to remember them. Once they'd evaporated, she was left with a lonely feeling of detachment.

Molly dreamt of a life away from here, away from the drugs, violence, her mum and Finchy. She'd had very little to start with in life, and knew that if she continued to stay here, that pattern would continue throughout adulthood. She didn't want to be like many of the mums on the estate, single, with kids in tow, living off donations from the food bank. Molly wanted to be far away from here in a small village in the middle of the country where no one knew her and no one could hurt her. She imagined walking along quaint, narrow cobbled streets where people smiled as she walked past, where local residents gathered at the church to support each other as a community, and the smell of freshly baked bread wafted from a bakery.

But for now, it was just a dream, nothing but a dream. She snuggled into the soft duvet and closed her eyes as it caressed her cheek. It still smelt of her grandma's house, that floral scent taking her back to Sunday afternoons knitting with the old lady. Molly hugged the duvet a little tighter and rolled over so it enclosed her in warmth.

That moment of peace and tranquillity was shattered as thoughts drifted into her mind of this afternoon. Hearing Finch and her drugged-up mum having sex in the next bedroom. He'd been aggressive, loud and forceful. Molly shuddered and tensed as she imagined what had unfolded in there. Her mum had stayed silent, and for her mum's sake, Molly hoped she'd been out of it and unaware of her body being violated. Molly felt her stomach twist and turn. Her heart raced as the realisation dawned that if she didn't do something soon, she would be next.

Molly's fingers curled into fists, her nails digging into each palm. She felt trapped and scared. Without Harry she'd be alone in this world.

She reached for the small mobile phone she kept hidden under her mattress. It was a cheap throwaway pay-as-you-go phone that Harry had given her to keep in touch with him. She only had one number stored… Harry's. She punched out a message.

Please come and get me… xx

Molly pulled herself from under the protection of her duvet and opened the door just a few inches as quietly as she could and peered through the small gap. She held her breath and listened. If Finch was still around, the last thing she wanted was for him to see her in just a T-shirt and a pair of knickers.

Certain the coast was clear, she tiptoed into the hallway and made her way towards the lounge. From the doorway, she could see her mum in her usual place, flopped on the sofa, dressed in nothing more than a dressing gown. The flimsy material gaped open, revealing that her mum wore nothing underneath. Her mum's face was washed out, wrinkled, and gaunt. The air was thick with the sickly sweet smell of weed.

"Mum."

"Mum!" Molly said again.

Her mum was out for the count. Molly suspected her mum wouldn't even know what day of the week it was, let alone what time it was. It was how her mum was most of the time.

Molly's stomach growled, and it was only then that she realised she hadn't eaten anything since breakfast this morning, two stale bits of toast and a glass of orange squash. She made her way to the kitchen and sighed at the mess. Discarded biscuit wrappers and empty tins littered the work surface, and plates and cups jostled each other for space in the sink. Molly tried at least once a week to tidy up after her mother and Finch, but fought a losing battle. She scrunched up her nose at the smell of rotting food and stale air.

Each cupboard she opened was bare. A few cheap tea bags, and half a bag of sugar were all she could find. She would have to settle for a few spoonfuls of sugar for energy to get through the rest of the evening.

She dipped back into the hallway and made her way back towards the bedroom, but froze when she heard snoring coming from her mum's bedroom.

Finch, shit.

She needed to make her escape before Finch woke, but she needed money and she knew where to get it.

But before that, she rushed to her bedroom and dressed, throwing off the bed T-shirt and slipping on her bra, Nike T-shirt and hoodie before slipping into a pair of skintight jeans, and lacing up her Converse trainers. If she had to run, she needed to be prepared to not look back or need anything. Harry would meet her around the corner, so she needed to move fast.

Molly turned the handle on her mum's bedroom door and pushed it ajar, being careful that the door hinges didn't squeak. As she peeked in, the smell of stale sweat, beer and more weed hit her. Bile rose as she bit down hard on her lips, the acid scorching her throat. She wanted to step away, but willed herself to push on and find what she needed. She tiptoed around in the darkness, her feet catching on discarded clothes and trainers that littered the floor.

Ever so gently, she pried open each drawer looking for the things she had seen when she had snooped around their bedroom on a previous occasion. There was nothing.

Has he taken it all away?

She glanced over her shoulder to check on Finch, her hands trembling. Her heart pounded so loud, she worried he could hear it. Molly licked her dry lips as she shivered. Tightness gripped her chest as if someone had their hands clasped around her throat.

Molly tiptoed towards the only wardrobe in the room. She tried to open the door, but it stuck, so she tugged again. It took a few moments for her to realise that clothes on the floor had caught beneath the bottom lip of the door. She pushed them away with the tip of a foot. The darkness made it hard to see much other than silhouettes of hanging clothes. She patted them down to see if there was anything stuffed in the pockets before dropping to her knees and rummaging around in all the bags thrown in the bottom. The plastic bags rustled as her hands brushed against them. She gasped and craned her neck around to see if he had heard her.

Another snore rattled deep inside Finch's throat. Then she found what she was looking for, a sports holdall with the zip undone. She plunged her hands into the bag and felt around, pulling out a large bundle of notes neatly folded in half. She grabbed as many as she could, stuffing them down the front of her jeans and into the pockets of her hoodie. There was more that she could feel, small squidgy bags, and then the cold kiss of metal which made her jerk her hand away.

Guilt flashed through her for a moment as she thought about the repercussions, and how Finch would take it out on her mum. She knelt what seemed like minutes undecided. Part of her wanted to leave the cash and run. But more of her wanted to take the money and create a new life with Harry. It would be enough to get them started and maybe rent a small flat while she looked for a job. She wasn't fussy. She would take anything, a cleaning job, working in a local Aldi or Lidl, or even distributing leaflets. It was the freedom she wanted more than anything else.

Her mind was made up. She would stick to her plan, and call the authorities once she'd gone so her mum would be released from a life of misery under Finch's control.

She retraced her steps out of the room, not looking back as she unlocked the front door and stepped out into the coolness of the evening. It wasn't until she was outside she realised that she'd been holding her breath for what felt like minutes. Her body felt drained, exhausted, and terrified. She was out here alone, destination unknown as she ran along the walkway and down the steps as fast as her legs would take her.

As she reached the bottom of the stairwell, she stopped, looking over her shoulder one last time. There was no turning back. It was time to take control of her life, and Harry had reassured her that he would take her away from all the pain and sadness that had blighted both of their lives. He reassured her that no one would ever hurt them again.

Molly made her way around to the side of the apartment block and made a break for freedom, heading towards the main exit of the estate where Harry would be waiting for her. She ran as fast as she could until she reached the main road. Just as she arrived, she froze on the spot as a convoy of police vehicles stormed past her and through the main entrance to the estate.

Hopefully they're there to take all the nasty scum off the estate, she thought as she walked away.

34

THE ELEMENT of surprise was more important now as Karen and the rest of the team pulled up close to the apartment block. Darkness brought with it a blanket of fear and vulnerability. The estate took on an icy chill despite the warmth of a June evening. Shadows were longer and darker, sounds were louder and clearer as the hum of background traffic had quietened to a faint murmur. The sound of a dog barking echoed around the buildings.

A group of youths, silhouetted in the dark, loitering close to the playground dispersed in random directions when the first car came into view.

They can well be part of Finch's gang, or lookouts, Karen thought.

Karen, Jade, Steve and Brad exited the first car. Two BMW X5 ARVs from SCO19, the specialist firearms command, split in different directions. One unit remained with Karen, while the other circled around towards the back of the apartment block to cover the rear exit. A personnel carrier followed towards the rear carrying eight officers dressed in dark overalls, body armour and protective helmets. It was an intimidating show of force, deliberate on Karen's part, to ensure Finch could be identified and secured safely. The extra officers would also ensure that any secondary disturbance could be quelled quickly and efficiently.

Several residents had gathered in the walkways of other apartment blocks. Some looked on in curiosity, others laughed and joked, and a few pockets of spectators jeered and heckled.

Karen knew their presence wouldn't be welcome, and the air was brittle with tension. Often raids of this nature created further friction between local communities and the police, but in Karen's eyes they were a necessity. With gang and knife crime so prevalent in London, the number of victims had grown exponentially. She knew some boroughs had council estates that were no-go areas for the police, or too unsafe and dangerous for any police officer to enter on their own or even twin crewed.

A big briefing beforehand meant everyone knew their specific role as Karen and her team followed behind the tactical entry team, their heavy boots and equipment sending vibrations through the floor as they made their way up the dingy stairwells. A distinct smell of weed lingered in the stairwells.

The advancing officers shuffled in a single line along the narrow walkway until they reached the apartment. Uniformed officers gathered either side, one burly officer stood facing the door, a big red enforcer in his hands. Two armed officers, one with a Heckler & Koch, the other with a SIG516, trained their weapons on the door. A further two officers stood either side, poised behind Perspex shields ready to barge through. Behind them the remaining officers formed an orderly line, each officer placing a hand on the shoulder of the officer in front so that they could move through in a methodical manner.

They waited for Karen's command. Due to the electric tension, the officers were tetchy. With the possibility of a firearm on the premises, Karen was in no mood to knock on the door waiting for an answer. She glanced around the estate one last time and saw the look of curiosity on the faces of residents before she gave the lead officer a nod.

"Go, go, go!!" she screamed.

The officer swung back the big red enforcer, and with all his might thrust it towards the door. The door offered little resistance The majority of council apartments had been made at minimal cost. The door frame and walls shook. Karen felt the vibration through her feet. The officer swung again, leaving the door hanging from its hinges.

"Police! Stay where you are! Police!" the firearms officers screamed as they surged through the opening, closely followed by the remaining officers shielded behind their Perspex protection. All officers were well-drilled with the shock and awe tactic. The element of surprise mixed with controlled aggression led to disorientation, which allowed officers vital seconds to gain the upper hand and bring the situation under control with minimal risk to themselves.

Darkness and silence greeted them as they stormed through the apartment. The armed officers cleared each room as they moved deeper into the flat. A commotion from the second bedroom led to more officers flooding the room.

Voices rose as a scuffle broke out. Screams and shouts echoed through the apartment as Karen and Jade waited in the hallway. Brad and Steve followed the other officers through to the lounge.

"Stay where you are! Don't move! Get him on the floor! Keep your hands where we can see them!"

Karen was in awe of her uniformed colleagues in such situations. Many days and months of training had led them to becoming the best officers in the world.

"Secure."

Having been given the all-clear, Karen proceeded into the room to find a dishevelled and dazed man face down on the bedroom floor, his arms secured behind his back with plastic cable ties.

"Darren Finch?" Karen asked as she knelt down.

Finch nodded, still groggy, drunk and half asleep.

"We need to ask you a few questions, and we have a warrant to search this premises."

"Boss!" Steve shouted from another room.

Karen found Steve in the lounge with an unresponsive female collapsed on the sofa. She was barely covered, and a female officer had been quick to throw a coat over the woman to maintain her dignity.

"I've called for an ambulance, but by the looks, she's out of it," Steve said, pointing towards the empty bottles of alcohol and used spliffs. The council had confirmed that the tenant's name was Angie Brennan, and for the time being, Karen had to assume that this was the woman's apartment. The council also confirmed that the woman was a single parent with a seventeen-year-old daughter called Molly.

Uniformed officers searched the flat while Karen started on Finch.

"Where were you six nights ago when Jack Taylor was murdered?"

"Who?" Finch replied, clearing his throat and licking his lips, his eyes rolling in their sockets.

"Jack Taylor, the guy who smacked you around, so don't say you don't know him. We've got it on the CCTV footage."

"No clue. You're wasting your time," Finch slurred.

Karen felt a burning urge to stomp on the man's head while he lay on the floor. For now he could sleep it off in the cells while he sobered up.

"Boss," Jade said as she walked towards Karen holding up a sports holdall found in the bottom of the wardrobe.

"Well, well, well. What have we here?" Karen said as she peered in. The holdall contained bundles of neatly folded twenty-pound notes, and large bags of a brown crumbly substance that Karen assumed was cannabis, a class B drug. There was far more than she'd expect for personal use. Possession and supply would carry at least a ten-year custodial, Karen hoped.

"That's not all," Jade added as she nodded in the direction of a firearms officer.

Karen turned to see the officer inspecting a handgun that he'd made safe.

"It was in the bag, boss," Jade continued.

Bingo!

It was a good result as far as Karen was concerned. Adding possession of a firearm to his litany of crimes, Finch wouldn't be coming out soon.

"We found this, too," Brad added as he came into the cramped quarters of the bedroom. Brad held up two brown paper evidence bags. "We found a machete and an axe behind the front door."

"This gets even better," Karen mused.

35

KAREN LEFT Jade to process Finch at the nearest police station. There was little that they could glean from him for the next few hours which offered forensics an opportunity to comb the flat for evidence that Karen could use in her interview. Brad accompanied Angie Brennan to the hospital and promised to update Karen as soon as doctors assessed her.

Despite wanting to go home and catch a few hours of sleep, she still had two important visits to make, both off the record. She made her way over to Mile End and to an address in Bancroft Road. Nestled between a long line of two-storey council apartment blocks was a small parade of shops. On the face of it, they looked no different to any other parade of shops found in the myriad of council estates across London. A sandwich bar, a food store, newsagent's and a chippy. There was nothing there to raise anyone's suspicion. Karen was far more interested in what was happening behind the chip shop. She found it ironic that the place she was visiting was opposite Mile End Hospital.

Karen ventured around to the side of the shops, and made her way towards the back door of the chip shop. It was a large steel reinforced door. She hammered on the cold steel with her fist. She waited a few moments before trying again.

"I'm coming. I'm coming," a voice came from inside along with the sound of approaching footsteps.

A short, bald man with grey stubble and closely set eyes in a chubby face answered the door. The smell of fried food swirled around them, and Karen's stomach responded with a hungry growl. She could murder a saveloy and chips.

The man looked her up and down, suspicion in his narrowed eyes.

"Yeah, can I help ya? I'm closed. Didn't you see the sign on the front door?" he asked with a tone of irritation.

Karen held up her warrant card. "I'm Detective Inspector Heath from the Metropolitan Police. You must be 'Two-tone' Charlie."

The man shook his head. "I don't know what you're talking about. There's no one here by that name."

Karen knew she had found the right man. He was called "Two-tone" Charlie because the man had a red and purple birthmark that covered part of his face from beneath his right eye down to the corner of his mouth and spread across his cheek to his right ear.

"Oh, I think you do," Karen replied barging in.

"Two-tone" Charlie protested. "Hold on a minute. You can't just waltz in here. I'm closed. You can come back tomorrow if you want chips."

Karen folded her arms as she looked around. "It's not your chips I'm interested in. It's what you have going on downstairs in the basement that's of interest."

"Two-tone" Charlie froze, his eyes wide like a deer caught in headlights, his lips bumbling incoherently. "There's just supplies down there. Tubs of oil, jars of pickle, stuff like that."

"Well, should we have a look down there?"

"Two-tone" Charlie shook his head. "I haven't got the keys on me."

Karen narrowed her eyes in mock surprise. "I would expect the keys to your basement are on the same bunch of keys that you use to lock up this place."

The man shifted on the spot.

Karen took a few steps to within a few inches of him. He took a few steps backwards and jammed himself up against the wall.

"We both know what you've got going on down there. It would only take a phone call and I could have a tactical firearms unit down there quicker than you can wipe your fat arse. Now, last time we paid you a visit, you had an illegal gun-making factory down there and you were supplying the Connells with their shooters."

The man's brow beaded with sweat, and his overweight frame struggled with a shortness of breath. He shook his head in denial.

"That's history. I learnt my lesson. I don't do that any more. I've gone straight."

Karen jabbed her fingers into his podgy chest. "I don't care if you've had tea with the Queen. I want a name for the job that happened nine months ago when two officers were gunned down. If someone needs a shooter for a job that big, we both know that you would be the first person that they would ask."

"Please. Please. I don't want any trouble. You know I can't say anything. I've not done anything like that in ages."

Karen smiled. "Sorry, chubby. I'm not buying that. You're not going to turn down a monkey if someone comes looking for a gun." She knew five hundred pounds was the going rate, and many criminals would pay even more for a clean weapon that hadn't been used.

"Two-tone" Charlie sobbed. "I'll be dead if I say anything."

Karen shrugged. "You'll be dead anyway. I only have to start spreading the word that you've been squealing like a pig. We'll be dragging your corpse out of the Thames in a matter of hours."

The man's eyes shifted from left to right as he considered his options, which at the moment he could count on one finger. "Adams," he blurted.

"Adams? What's his first name?"

"I dunno. I had a phone call to prepare two shooters. I don't know who called me, and I didn't ask, either. I was just told that a bloke called Adams would come by and drop off a couple of bags of sand."

"Bags of sand?" Karen questioned, looking perplexed. She knew a little slang from the East End, but a bag of sand was a new one on her.

"Bag of sand. A grand."

Karen rolled her eyes. "How many bags?"

"Three."

"And what did that give them?"

"Two sawn-offs, and a handgun. All clean."

Karen took a description of the man known as Adams before she left and stepped out on to the pavement. It wasn't until she got around to the front of the block that she leant back against the brick wall and took large breaths to calm her racing heart. She had taken a big risk going there alone. But she had a name now.

THE BROOMFIELD RESIDENTIAL Care Home was a small unit that cared for less than a dozen patients. It had a softer feel to it than a normal hospital ward. The corridors were carpeted, the individual rooms were tastefully decorated, and the families could personalise each room with ornaments and pictures to make the stay of their loved ones as comfortable as possible.

Karen was greeted by Robyn Allen, the nurse she'd spoken to earlier in the evening. Nurse Allen had a kind and soft face. Her brown hair was pulled back in a ponytail, and she wore a blue tunic and dark navy trousers. She greeted Karen with a hug in much the same way as meeting a long-lost friend.

They exchange pleasantries. Robyn was clearly delighted to see Karen as she bombarded her with questions about her job, and what she'd been up to.

Though Karen appreciated the welcome, it was overwhelming just being there. After the day she'd had, she was tired and just wanted some peace and quiet with her sister.

Karen eventually pulled herself away from the nurse and made her way to her sister's room. There was a stillness and a sense of calm as she stepped through the doorway. It was in marked contrast to the hustle and bustle and frenetic pace of her job. She moved towards her sister and stood by her bed. She reached out and held her sister's hand. It was warm, thin and bony.

"Hi, Jane. It's me, Big Sis. Sorry I haven't been in a while, it's been *sooo* manic."

Even though her sister was asleep, she felt a rush of guilt as the words tripped from her lips. Her sister was asleep during most of her visits. Occasionally, she would open her eyes and stare at Karen without blinking. There was an emptiness in Jane's eyes, no expression, no feeling, and no hint as to what she might be experiencing. Karen hoped that Jane was pleased to see her on the rare occasions of her visits, even if she couldn't tell. She had sat there for many hours in the past, wondering exactly what her sister was feeling. Was she sad? Was she in pain? *Did she experience pain?* Did she know what it felt like to feel sad?

Karen would never know the answers. But she hoped Jane found comfort and happiness at some level each time she saw her big sister.

Jane was thin with sunken cheekbones and limbs commonly associated with someone in their eighties. A lack of movement had left her with little to no muscle and a fragility that sometimes made Karen scared to touch her.

Karen pulled up a chair and dropped herself into it with a sigh as she flipped her head back and enjoyed the softness of the fabric. She took a few moments to just watch her little sister before she told Jane about what she had been up to recently. She told her about Manky's antics, and what was happening in the world. It was a one-sided conversation, and Karen wondered if Jane got bored of hearing her voice and the inconsequential mutterings from a frayed and fractious mind.

It saddened her to see how differently their lives had turned out. The shock of seeing her little sister when they were younger had left deep psychological scars. Scars she ignored or denied. Deep down she knew it was one reason she was a commitment-phobe. What happened if she settled down with someone and started a family? Was there a risk that her children might suffer complications at birth? She knew it was foolish to think that way, but she couldn't help herself.

She could barely look after herself, so what chance did she have of looking after her own children? She often looked at children and babies and didn't feel that maternal tug that so many women spoke about. To her, babies were nothing more than crying and pooping machines. And as they grew older became nothing more than trouble as they bled you dry of every single penny.

Maybe she was just a cynical old bitch, and too long in the tooth.

She sat in silence for another hour, looking at her sister and enjoying the stillness in her mind before she got up, kissed her sister gently on the forehead, and stroked her cheek. She watched her sister's chest rise and fall with each breath.

"I promise I won't leave it so long next time," she whispered. Whether she could stick to that promise only she could tell, but the guilt for not coming sooner sat heavy on her chest.

She glanced over her shoulder as she stood in the doorway and offered the smallest of smiles before she headed off into the night.

Exhaustion slumped her shoulders. The pillows had been fluffed, the temperature in the room perfect, even her favourite night light had been on. But no matter how hard she'd tried, she just couldn't get to sleep. She'd stared at the ceiling. Nothing. Giving up on sleep, she finally heated a cup of milk and added a pinch of cinnamon to it before settling on the sofa.

After finishing the last few drops of the creamy, frothy liquid, Karen slipped on her fluffy carpet slippers, left the cup on the coffee table and scurried back to bed. Her insomnia had not worn off as she tossed and turned, swore under her breath, punched the pillow to get comfortable, before the god of slumber, Hypnos, blessed her with an hour's sleep.

36

Karen was in early. She'd caught one of the first Central Line trains from Epping. With it being the start of the line, it guaranteed her a seat which she needed today.

The duty sergeant confirmed that Finch had slept all night and was beginning to stir. They would give him tea and a bacon sandwich before starting the interview process.

"You did well last night," Skelton said as he stepped into her office. "It looks like your gamble paid off."

Karen nodded. "Yes. It was a good result. Forensics worked through the night and I should get a ballistics report any moment to see if the gun we recovered is linked to either murder. And the icing on the cake would be if they've identified any gunshot residue on the clothes we recovered from his bedroom."

"Either way, it looks like Finch isn't going anywhere. Any update on the Brennan woman?"

"Brad was with her for a few hours last night. She's stable but disorientated. Based on what the doctors said, it sounds like booze and drugs were all she lived on. They're organising additional support services to visit her as soon as she's fit to talk. Brad will be back there at some point to see if we can get a statement from her. The more evidence we can get against Finch, the stronger our case."

Karen stood and came around from behind her desk in readiness to check on Finch. "I heard from the duty sergeant we had further firearms incidents last night. Shots were fired in several locations in Shoreditch."

Skelton nodded. "Yeah, I heard. It kept the firearms boys busy. Give me an update once you've spoken to Finch. I need to head out for a meeting." He smiled. "I understand that the Brennan woman had a daughter living with her? Any sign of her?"

"No. Her stuff is there, but there was no sign of her. Brad couldn't get anything out of the mum regarding her daughter's whereabouts. So she's unaccounted for."

"Probably dossing elsewhere, a mate's maybe?"

"Maybe, but she's also vulnerable considering her home life. I've alerted officers to keep an eye out for her in case she returns."

Skelton had a thumping headache. They had instructed him to make himself visible in public places. He'd headed to a bar in Moorgate where he had chatted to those who served him. He'd made sure he was in full view of the CCTV inside the bar, especially when he'd started to chat to a few women who were on a night out. Skelton had then made his way to a casino for a few hours before picking up a takeaway from the fried chicken shop on his way home. In every location, he'd made sure he glanced towards the CCTV cameras.

As she breezed down the corridor, a notepad and case file in one hand, and a mug of coffee in the other, Karen confirmed she would call him as soon as she had any significant updates. Her mind buzzed with all the things that she wanted to quiz Finch about. She wanted to check her theory that Finch may have killed Taylor in revenge. But another thought bothered her. She could see why Finch may have killed Taylor, but that didn't explain the connection to Macholl's murder, if there was one.

Jade waited outside the interview room as Karen approached.

"How is our guest?" Karen asked.

"Sounds like shit and looks like shit. He's tetchy." Jade smirked.

"Perfect. Has he got legal representation?"

Jade nodded. "Duty solicitor. Marc Jacobs."

Karen knew the name. He was one of several duty solicitors they contacted when a suspect didn't have their own solicitor. Jacobs was a quiet man. But his demeanour was misleading as she had known Jacobs to turn in an instant as he challenged officer's questions. Karen opened the door and strode into the room, chest puffed out, shoulders back. With the pleasantries done and the formal caution stated for the benefit of the recorder, Karen took a few moments to glance at Finch.

Finch had a round chubby face and a heavy, stubbly beard. He had short, dark brown hair with matching dark brown and bloodshot eyes. From this distance Karen smelt his putrid breath that reeked of alcohol and tobacco. He sat in a white paper suit that rustled each time he moved. He had his hands on the table, his fingers interlocked. Finch looked thoroughly bored and wasted.

Karen smiled again at Jacobs, thinking he looked intellectual. He had glasses, they were round frames very much in the style of Harry Potter's, and dark, curly hair. Though his hair was shorter, he reminded Karen of Leo Sayer, a singer from the eighties.

"Darren Finch, how did you come to be in possession of a gun we found in your wardrobe?" Karen asked, sliding across the table a picture taken of the sports bag and handgun.

Finch looked across to the duty solicitor and then turned and smiled. "No comment."

"Who supplied you with the gun?"

"No comment."

Most suspects she interviewed gave the typical standard reply. Remaining silent and offering nothing more than a "no comment" reduced their risk of accidentally saying something that would incriminate them.

Karen switched direction, her eyes locked on him. "It must have been embarrassing when Taylor gave you a good kicking in front of your mates? Knocked you down a peg or two? Made you feel like a little man?"

Finch's eyes flickered and twitched, as the muscles in his cheeks flexed.

Karen knew she'd hit a raw nerve. "Is that why you put a bullet through his head?"

"No comment."

"I think you were so humiliated, especially on your own patch, that you had no alternative but to settle a score with him. What do you think, Finch?"

Finch remained silent, his eyes locked in a battle of aggression with hers. His fingers clenched, his knuckles turning white.

Karen turned towards Jade. "You see, sergeant, once forensics have confirmed gunshot residue on his clothing, and all the other evidence is presented to him, he'll be charged with two murders, and looking at least fifteen years, maybe even longer."

Jade nodded. "Possibly even twenty years."

Karen looked back towards Finch. "It's difficult being banged up for so long. Twenty-three hours a day of staring at grey peeling walls, hearing inmates crying, even screaming, and looking over your shoulder constantly, wondering if you're about to become someone's bitch. Especially when the other inmates find out you broke the code of silence, honour amongst thieves and all that crap."

Finch slammed his hands on the table. "That's bullshit. You know that's lies, and I can have you done for that."

Her remarks created the reaction she had hoped for.

Steve's knock on the door interrupted the interview. Karen suspended the interview and excused herself from the room. She was gone less than sixty seconds before she re-entered and took a seat. Jade started the tape recorder again, confirming those present in the room before Karen continued.

Karen remained silent for a few moments just letting the tension simmer. Finch glanced at Karen for a brief moment before looking away.

"Darren Finch, you are in a very difficult situation now."

Karen's sombre tone caused Finch to shift in his chair as he glanced back and forth between Karen and Jade.

"We've just had the ballistics report back from the handgun found in your wardrobe. The prints are a match for yours. But I've now had it confirmed the handgun was used in the murders of Jack Taylor and Dean Macholl. It was also used to violently assault a manager at a convenience store six days ago."

Finch's temples throbbed as the anger boiled inside him. Sensing it, Jacobs placed a hand on Finch's arm to placate him.

"Inspector, just because the weapon was used to murder two people, it doesn't place my client at either crime scene. He may merely have been holding on to it for someone else, and until you can prove that my client was present, you are merely speculating."

Finch threw off Jacobs's hand. "It wasn't me. I haven't shot anyone. I don't even know who this Dean Macholl fella is." Finch exploded from his seat and kicked his chair back as he slammed his fist on the table. Karen and Jade recoiled to give themselves enough space to react if he launched himself in their direction. A uniformed officer who was present rushed forward and pushed Finch back in his seat, restraining him till he calmed down.

"I'm telling you I had nothing to do with either murder. You are way off the mark."

Karen pushed some still images across the table that showed the altercation between Finch and Taylor, as well as timed stills of Finch and his gang leaving just before Taylor's murder and returning not long after.

"It doesn't look good, does it?"

Finch held his hands up and smiled to worm his way out of the situation. "Listen, yeah, you can see from the photographs that me and Taylor had a run-in. I'd been running his drugs, but I got greedy, and skimmed some cash for myself. Taylor found out and came to give me a hiding. He wanted his money back."

"So you thought it would be easier to shoot him than pay back what you owed?"

Finch shook his head. "Don't be daft. I might take a few risks, but I wouldn't go head-to-head with Taylor. Not many would. He's a nutter."

"So maybe you paid someone else to kill Jack?"

"No. No. No. Taylor gave me a hiding, big deal. He wanted his money back, and the only way for me to do that quickly was to go and rip off the convenience store. That's where we were heading," Finch said, poking some photographs with his finger. He carried on to describe the store, the amount of money they'd stolen, a clear description of the manager, and where Finch had hit him.

The revelation wasn't something that Karen needed. Even though footage of the bookies had failed to provide detailed descriptions of the assailants, DNA found on the butt of the handgun linked the weapon to the crime.

For a moment Karen had to consider that Finch could be off the hook.

37

SKELTON MADE his way over to the small commercial unit near the Wilson Industrial Estate. It took him a while to find it from the instructions Sally had given him. When he arrived, half a dozen stocky men congregated by the side of three Range Rovers parked in a line. A feeling of intimidation and aggression crackled in the air as they turned to see Skelton pull up and exit his car. The men stiffened, and formed a makeshift line, an impenetrable human barrier that even the England rugby team would have struggled to plough through.

Due to their shaved heads, stubbly beards, and bulky tops, Skelton felt the hairs on the back of his neck stand on end. They eyed him with suspicion as he walked towards them. If he hoped that they would part to one side to allow him through, he was mistaken as he stopped inches from them. His eyes narrowed as he glanced from one to another, holding his ground. Though his insides twisted with adrenaline, he gritted his teeth unwilling to be intimidated by such a show of force.

Sally and her brothers emerged from the unit and approached the back of the crowd.

“I see you brought the ballet squad with you, Sal,” Skelton quipped. He hadn’t shifted his eyes from staring down the men.

Terry and Steve Connell stepped around from behind their sister and made their way towards Skelton, their hands curled in iron-like fists, ready to mete out their own style of justice.

Sally smiled. “Boys, now now. No need to get your hands dirty on a nice day like this. He’s just tugging your chain.”

The Connell brothers paused mid-step, hatred contorting their faces. They puffed their chests out like centurions storming into battle. Terry snarled.

Despite being outnumbered, Skelton enjoyed baiting the men though he would have been powerless to do anything had they turned on him. Knowing Sally was there afforded him protection. He knew he was treading a fine line, but enjoyed the attention and the thrill. It was the same feeling he had when he gambled, though he hated how we felt afterwards, especially when he lost.

Sally stepped through the crowd of Neanderthals towards Skelton and planted a kiss on his lips. The Connell brothers bristled with anger as their sister teased them.

Sally turned and stared at the men behind her. She smirked before she walked straight towards and through them as the group of men parted. She loved taunting them. It was a trait she had inherited from her father who had taunted both his enemies and those who worked for him. And now Sally enjoyed it, too.

Skelton knew Sally was playing with him, but he was weak… for her.

"This way, Skelton," she barked as she made her way towards the unit.

Skelton followed a few yards behind her as the men hemmed him in. The group made their way to the unit.

It was a huge unit. One wall was filled with boxes stacked ten-foot high. To the right there was a long table, about eight-foot long with three boxes on it.

Sally opened the lid of one box and pulled out a large pile of cash, a combination of twenties and fifties. She fanned through the notes before throwing them in Skelton's direction. She shot him a cursory look as if money bored her.

Skelton's eyes lit up as he caught it.

"You've done well recently, so this is a little bonus for you. There's five grand there. Don't spend it all on booze and lap dancers."

Skelton should have been pleased, but his heart sank when he realised he would be giving back a fair portion to pay off debts to her brothers.

Sally reached into the second box and pulled out a small, clear plastic package. It looked like nothing more than a bag of flour. She grabbed a small Stanley knife from the table, and cut a small hole in the bag before emptying some of the contents. Steve Connell pushed his way towards the table. He reached into his pocket and pulled out a twenty-pound note which he rolled into a thin tube-like shape. He placed one end of the makeshift tube against one nostril before leaning forward and placing the other end towards the edge of the white powder.

With his free hand he pressed down on the other nostril before inhaling some loose powder. He stood up and shook his head before turning to Sally and nodding.

Sally looked towards Skelton and held her stare for a few seconds. "Well, what you waiting for? Your turn."

Skelton offered the smallest of smiles as he stepped forward and took the rolled twenty-pound note from Steve. He glanced at the group, and not wanting to back down from a challenge, he clamped one nostril shut before placing the tube against the other and doing the same.

Skelton stood and inhaled, his chest rising as he closed his eyes. He waited for that feeling to kick in. It was more pleasant and relaxing than IVing it where you got a BANG! He found that too harsh. When he snorted, he would get a *mmmm* kind of feeling and a flood of euphoria.

Sally offered the slightest of sly smiles before she reached into the box and grabbed another identical package and tossed it in Skelton's direction. "Use it, sell it, or stick it up your arse, whatever grabs your fancy. My gift to you."

Skelton knew it was a gift but another way to keep him tied to their organisation.

"Thanks."

Sally reached into the third box. It was much smaller, but bristling with over a dozen handguns. Sally grabbed the first one that came to hand and examined it like it was a beautiful piece of fine china. "We've got a problem."

The air turned thick with tension as doubt swept across Skelton's mind.

"Heath. She's a liability. She's been asking more questions again. It's come to our attention she paid 'Two-tone' Charlie a visit looking for names."

"And did Charlie give her a name?"

"Yes. He said Adams."

"I've got her under control." Skelton tried to pacify her.

Skelton didn't see the fist from his peripheral vision as it connected with the side of his head, sending his body crashing to the floor. The hard and cold concrete floor sent shock waves of pain through his body as he landed on his back. His head bounced off the floor with a sickening thud. Dazed and confused, he made out the blurry outline of Terry lurching over him, a fist pulled back close to his shoulder ready to strike Skelton again. Skelton was in trouble. His legs felt like jelly. His head pounded and for a brief moment he thought he was going to throw up or shit himself.

The sound of Sally's heels clicking across the floor dazed his senses further as she levelled up close to his head and knelt down.

"You see, we have a problem. And I don't like problems. My brothers don't like problems." She tapped the muzzle against the side of Skelton's cheek. "You are close to being a liability. You don't have her under control, so stop bullshitting me."

"I promise; I will sort it," Skelton replied, his mind dazed, his voice croaky. Skelton had told Heath to back off, and asking her to do it again would raise further suspicion.

The corner of Sally's mouth curled up in a wry smile. "Either you do, or we'll arrange for *Detective Inspector*

Karen Heath to come to an unfortunate end off a bridge over the M25. We've done it before to coppers, and we'll do it again. Understand?"

Skelton offered the smallest of nods. "And what about Adams and 'Two-tone' Charlie?" Skelton asked, licking his dry lips as the pain intensified inside his head. It felt like someone had hit him with a sledgehammer.

"We'll take care of our loose ends. Don't you worry about that."

Skelton understood her meaning and probed no further. As he glanced around, his eyes focused again on the men staring back with dark and blank expressions.

Sally looked up and down her asset. The dusty concrete floor had left a grey tinge to Skelton's navy suit. "Now get out of here and get yourself cleaned up, because you look like a sack of shit."

38

Karen paced around her office frustrated with the outcome of the interview. The case was building against Finch, but her gut instinct told her that something was missing. She had spent the last hour reviewing every scrap of evidence, every statement, and crunching through her own theories.

Forensics had confirmed that Finch's prints were lifted from a phone belonging to the manager of the convenience store. Making a fatal error, Finch had removed one of his gloves during the raid. The ballistics report had confirmed that the gun retrieved from Finch's apartment had been used in the murder of Jack Taylor and Dean Macholl, so she could at least get him for possession. And yet something gnawed away in her mind.

She could link Finch and Taylor. They were connected in business, and it was plausible that Finch went after Taylor in revenge. But the loose piece of the puzzle was Macholl. No matter how hard she tried, she couldn't find a connection between Finch and Macholl. There was no evidence of them working together, being affiliated together, or having a run-in. Was there an angle she was missing?

The confines of the office stifled her thinking. She needed space to focus and a change of scenery. Karen grabbed her mobile phone and told Jade she was popping out for a few moments, and to call her straightaway if anything important came through.

Karen slipped out of the office and into the stream of people passing back and forth along the street. She didn't have any direction in which to walk. She needed to feel normal, but questioned what normal actually meant. Her life had been a whirlwind of ups and downs, pressure, sleepless nights, long hours at work and bucketloads of stress.

A coffee shop down a side street caught her attention and she ducked inside. She ordered a cappuccino and a Danish pastry and found a quiet corner. It was one of those trendy coffee shops with a more relaxed feel, featuring couches and armchairs. It reminded her of the place where the characters in *Friends* the TV series used to hang out, Central Perk. She sank into an armchair; it was one of those wing-back chairs with a high back. It felt warm and snuggly as she pushed her head back and blew out a loud sigh.

She was tired of the job. Her career had been thriving until nine months ago, and following the ambush and return to work, she felt she had to prove herself over again. A blemish on her career, that's what it was. Wherever she went, whichever station, whichever office or whenever she attended a meeting, she knew people were looking at her, questioning her capabilities and wondering if she truly did feel remorse.

If she was honest with herself, it pissed her off big time. She had considered the next steps in her career, and being a DCI had been taken away from her. Now she wondered if that would ever be possible to get back there again. The process was long and drawn out, and she was certain that additional questions would be raised during the selection process regarding that event nine months ago.

She held her large cappuccino in both hands as she sipped at it and glanced around the café. She noticed two women huddled in one corner, out of the way. Karen put them in their late twenties, possibly early thirties. They were smiling and exchanging laughs as they listened to each other's stories. They looked relaxed; they looked happy. Their skin looked smooth and free of worry lines. She wondered what they did for jobs, what their lives were like, and whether they had worries that bogged them down.

More than anything else, Karen wanted her reputation back. Her own behind-the-scenes investigation had been unproductive. The Connells had to be involved. They wouldn't allow another firm to come on to their patch and commit such an act without their approval. But every lead she chased led to an impenetrable wall of silence. People were ignorant or too scared to say anything.

The Commissioner had ordered a review into the transportation and protection of key witnesses in major trials following the ambush, and her actions had instigated the review. Only a handful of people had known they were moving Anne, so the most plausible explanation was an inside job. A mole. A betrayal of the oath to protect and serve. Perhaps it had been one of the officers who lost their lives? Maybe the ambush had been botched? Maybe the mastermind had planned on injuring officers to make it look realistic? If that was the case, she would never know.

At the time, the internal investigation had reviewed and interviewed every single member of the team to identify any weak links. None were found. That part baffled her more than anything else. It had to be the Connells, but they seem to be one step ahead of her. There had to be a mole in the force, and despite the initial finger of suspicion being pointed at her, she had fought tooth and nail to rebuff that particular accusation.

Karen stared through the glass window of the café at the cars and vans that passed by.

A mole?

There could be only one possibility she hadn't yet considered, the DCI. But surely that couldn't be the case? She did have doubts about him. He was always telling her to forget any investigation into the Connells. He often didn't support her in her decisions, and to top it off, was a lecherous tosser.

Karen acknowledged that she'd have to investigate, but her mind turned towards her current efforts and the many unanswered questions she had. Reviewing the CCTV footage again would be her next step. There had to be more they were missing. She finished her remaining cappuccino and realised she hadn't started the Danish pastry while so deep in thought. She wrapped it in a serviette and decided to have it later.

The women she had watched earlier were still laughing and smiling, deep in conversation as she left.

Sometimes life seemed so unfair.

39

Karen returned to the office and made herself a cup of coffee before catching up with the team and getting the latest updates.

She sat at her desk and nibbled on her Danish pastry. Karen cursed herself for not picking up a sandwich while she was out because she was both hungry and tired. She hoped the quick carb fix would help her to power through.

She opened the case files and then closed them seconds later with a sigh. She had looked through them, and analysed every element just hours ago and doubted that looking at them again would reveal any new facts. It felt like she was just spinning her wheels. There was something she was missing and felt that the motives behind the killings went back further than just the past few weeks and months.

Karen's mind drifted to a conversation she'd had with Diane a few days ago. She'd questioned the woman about the history between Taylor and Macholl and what transpired to be a crude love triangle. It was an angle she hadn't explored much. She'd overlooked it, preferring instead to focus on recent events. Had that been where she'd gone wrong?

Reaching for her mouse, she opened a few screens on her computer and pulled up historical information relating to Macholl's past. As far as she could tell, everything was okay until the botched raid on the bookies six years ago. Opening another screen, she pulled up records relating to the raid on the Paddy Power bookmakers. Karen spent the next hour reviewing the forensic reports, witness statements, and the investigating officer's notes before picking up the phone and dialling a number.

Just over an hour later, Karen arrived at Kingston police station. She noticed that Kingston High Street was much quieter and more suburban in feel compared to London. A mixture of old and new buildings, independent stores and smaller chains, along with charming pedestrianised streets, offered a relaxed atmosphere. She stopped on the Clattern Bridge and peered over the edge at the Hoggsmill River that flowed beneath its arch and snaked its way through the town before joining up with the Thames.

The police station had the same features as most police stations in the Met. A large, ageing grey monstrosity, skirted on the ground floor by blue window frames.

Detective Inspector Andrew Morton greeted Karen at reception. He was a slender man, receding on top, with an angular jawline. Dressed in a navy suit with a garish pink tie and white shirt, he led Karen through to his office on the second floor. She was surprised at how small the room was in comparison to hers. It was cluttered with just enough room for his desk, chair, and two visitor's chairs.

"Thanks for taking the time to see me. I needed to pick your brain about an old case."

Morton shrugged. "Happy to help in whichever way I can. Although, I'm sure we could have done this over the phone?"

Karen nodded and agreed. "Absolutely. But to be honest it's sometimes nice to get out and meet other colleagues, and I thought this was something that was worth discussing face-to-face."

Karen took a few moments to get Morton up to speed. She spoke about the two murder cases, and how she was going round in circles and missing the obvious.

"I'm struggling with the motives. I know the two men were associated and then they had a falling out. But from what I can gather, they've had no contact over the past five years while Macholl was in prison. So I'm thinking there must be a historical element to this, and I wanted to find out more about the Paddy Power case?"

Morton rolled his eyes. "I remember the case well. It was a right pain in the arse. We knew who did it, but the evidence was thin on the ground, and CPS wasn't buying it. Taylor and Macholl were definitely involved; we even had informants confirm that. Taylor was in charge, and he ran the job."

Karen listened as Morton recalled the salient points around the investigation. None of it was new, and frustration ate at her until Morton revealed a new and vital piece of information.

After Elaine Atkin's death, the police discovered that following the analysis of her phone messages they had promised her a share from the raid. Where the messages came from hadn't been discovered, and police at the time put it down to a burner phone. Who the phone belonged to remained a mystery, but suspicion had fallen on Taylor because Elaine Atkin's had been dating him.

Karen listened intently as Morton went off on a tangent for a few moments. He reflected on the fallout from the raid and the fact that a young, single mum had been manipulated by Taylor. Ultimately, she'd paid the price with her life. Karen picked up on a bitterness in Morton's tone.

They discussed the case for a while longer, and bandied about motives and theories, before Karen thanked him for his time and made her way back to Shoreditch.

As she walked past Skelton's office, Karen did a double take. The man had his head buried in his hands, and his elbows resting on his desk. Just a few hours ago Skelton had been wearing a navy suit, and was now wearing a grey one. A shiver of surprise settled in her chest. She knocked on his door and waited for him to wave her in. She was taken aback by what appeared to be slight bruising to the side of his face. Sensing that Skelton had noticed her looking, she drew her eyes back level with his.

"Yes?" Skelton asked bluntly.

"Um, um… you've changed your suit…" Karen offered as she pointed towards him.

"Ten out of ten for observation skills, Karen."

Karen waited for an explanation, and when one wasn't forthcoming, she continued to fill the silence. She updated him on the meeting with DI Morton over in Kingston, and her new focus of attention. Despite sounding positive and encouraged by her visit, Karen couldn't help notice how Skelton appeared more jittery than usual. His phone rested on the desk, and his eyes kept drifting to it, as if expecting a message or urgent phone call.

Come to think of it, Karen thought he looked far worse than normal. His face looked haggard and tired, the slight bruising only adding to his untidy look and his weary frame. He was present, but not present.

"Sir, are you okay?" she asked.

When Skelton didn't reply, she asked again, jolting the man from his thoughts.

Skelton nodded and stood up, confirming that the one-sided conversation was over.

Everything about Skelton worried her. His ethics, his lifestyle, and his true intentions. He should be at home, enjoying retirement and the generous police pension, but he remained on the job. Wanting to probe further, Karen questioned him.

"It's getting late now, sir. Have you got any plans for this evening? Or are you having a lazy one?"

Skelton shook his head. "No plans. You?"

"Not sure yet, sir. I'll probably hang around here for a little longer. I've got a few things I want to check out."

Skelton's phone buzzed with the news of an incoming text message. He grabbed his phone and read the message before grabbing his suit jacket from the back of his chair. Jostling Karen out of his office, he made his way for the stairs.

40

SKELTON'S suspicious behaviour piqued Karen's interest as she waited a few moments before heading down the stairwell. Her mind turned over the many possibilities that clouded her thinking. Was Skelton a loose cannon? Had the job taken its toll on him after all these years, leaving him weary, anxious and hard-nosed? Or was he on the verge of having a breakdown?

She stepped out on to the pavement and dipped in behind all the commuters heading home for the evening. She could make out Skelton about twenty yards ahead, ambling towards the Tube station. Small plumes of grey smoke billowed into the air as he puffed hard on a cigarette, keen to finish it before heading into the Tube station.

Chasing away the annoying voice of reason, she sidestepped into a doorway as Skelton slowed. He stood to one side of the pavement, working his way through his stick of poison and watching people walk by.

After a few moments, Skelton threw the butt on the floor and extinguished it with the sole of his shoe.

Karen followed him into the station, and down to the platform. She stood behind a large, burly man, hoping he would shield her from Skelton's prying eyes. As the train arrived, she got on to the next carriage, but close enough to allow her to maintain eye contact.

They rode the train for seven stops before Skelton alighted, hotly followed by Karen. She maintained visual contact by focusing on his head as he weaved in and out of the throng of commuters, up the escalators, and through the ticket barriers.

By the time Karen had reached street level, Skelton had lit another cigarette and walked away. Karen wondered where he was going. She knew where he lived, but he seemed to walk in random directions, heading down streets that ran in the opposite direction to where he should have been heading. Curiosity ate away at her. He appeared to be in a world of his own, ambling along with no destination in mind, in marked contrast to his hurried exit from the office.

The sound of commuter traffic, car horns blaring, and the general hum of city life quietened as the minutes rolled by. They moved deeper into the network of residential streets. Karen felt the first sign of nerves creeping in. The further they walked, the fewer people she had to hide behind. If Skelton walked for much longer, it would just be the two of them in the street and she'd have to drop back further and risk losing him.

She wondered if this had been a fruitless exercise. She had to find out more about Skelton, but following him on a whim seemed foolish now. What was she thinking?

She watched as Skelton crossed over the road and disappeared into a small off-licence that nestled between two houses. Karen waited a minute or two, inching closer, before she found herself feet away from the glass frontage. She willed herself to walk away, fearing Skelton could walk out and catch her. Her thoughts abandoned her as she wondered what pathetic excuse she could come up with. But something inside pushed her on, a side of her that sought the truth.

As if an invisible force had pushed her with two hands, she stared through the glass windows. She watched Skelton pay for some cigarettes and a prepackaged meal before turning to leave.

Karen gasped and darted away from the window into the nearest doorway. She held her breath, hoping and pleading that Skelton wouldn't walk past her. A sigh of relief escaped her lips as he walked off in the other direction. She waited until there was a sizeable distance between them before she continued.

Skelton headed back towards his house, and ten minutes later put the key in the door and shut it behind him.

Karen blew out her cheeks in frustration. She had been on a wild goose chase and cursed herself under her breath. "Bloody idiot."

Sitting on the edge of the pavement between two cars for over an hour, lost in her thoughts didn't help Karen at all. A mixture of embarrassment and frustration seeped from her pores. She wasn't sure what she had hoped to gain by following him. Answers perhaps? Proof?

But tailing the man hadn't brought her peace of mind. She didn't feel better, and returned to her apartment in Epping. She was too tired to do anything, her mind racing in turmoil. She settled for a few slices of toast with jam and a cup of tea in front of the TV. With Manky by her feet, purring with delight that his mummy was home, Karen flicked through her recorded TV programmes. Even though her eyes were glued to the screen, she couldn't digest it. Her mind drifted along, unsure which direction to take next.

Skelton rarely found himself in Sally's bed so late at night, but she'd caught him by surprise with a late-night call. And if he was honest, he needed her. Finally around midnight, he'd left his house to meet her.

Watching through the closed curtains in his darkened room, Skelton had watched as Karen sat between two cars, looking like a miserable, homeless down-and-out. He waited a further hour after she had left before he slipped out of the door and made his way to Sally's.

Sally had wanted to discuss business before moving on to pleasure. She'd told Skelton that they had some new girls coming in from Lithuania, and she needed Skelton to check out the police activity around the location. Skelton was told to find out what intelligence the police had gathered on prostitution rings close to the address. He reassured her he would make the necessary enquiries.

He smiled to himself as he stared up at the ceiling while Sally ducked under the covers to pleasure him. He loved her sexual appetite.

Euphoria washed over him as she teased him with her tongue. His body jerked, his heart raced, and he throbbed with ecstasy. But his mind flicked back to Karen as he recalled the events of this evening. He had played along with her games, leading her on a merry dance. He couldn't believe how stupid she'd been to follow him. Her surveillance tactics were piss poor in his opinion. He almost burst out laughing when he recalled standing in the off-licence, and glancing at the CCTV monitor behind the counter. Karen lurked outside looking at him through the glass picture window.

Karen would have to try harder.

Sally snapped him back to the present as she emerged from under the covers and positioned herself astride of him. "Now for round two," she cooed.

41

Like she did most mornings, Karen made herself a coffee in the office kitchen and strolled back to her office. On this occasion, she sat in silence just staring at a blank computer screen for over an hour. Most of the team weren't in yet. Apart from Jade, who had popped her head around the corner just to say hi.

It was one of those mornings where she couldn't shake off the melancholy. It came and went, often without reason or warning, and today was one of those days. It left her feeling nothing. Empty.

Karen wished she knew why, but whenever she stopped to examine her feelings, she found no plausible reasons as to why her mood plummeted faster than the Tower of Terror ride at Disney.

"Pull yourself out of this. Come on. You've got to do this," she whispered to herself. She shook her head, flexed her fingers, and willed herself to get her arse in gear.

Karen came back to the CCTV footage of the estate, and the restaurant on the night that Macholl had turned up. She reviewed the tapes, repeating several times, stopping at random points whenever she saw figures appear on the screen. With the Taylor and Macholl files open, she cross-referenced every detail once again. She watched the video as Macholl arrived at the restaurant and saw nothing that concerned her.

Karen rewound the tape to the beginning and watched a host of diners, general members of the public, turn up at the restaurant. The two large, burly minders arrived and took up their position by the front door. She let the tape run while she pulled the list of attendees from the file. Karen ticked them off one by one against the list of attendees. It started with some of Taylor's associates before friends and family arrived. Taylor arrived suitably late, arm in arm with Diane, and Ben trailing a few feet behind.

Karen noticed that Ben's body language suggested he wasn't happy. His hands were stuffed in his trouser pockets, and his head was slightly tipped forward.

She paused and examined the last two names, Harry Coleman and Molly Brennan. Karen continued to run the tape, waiting for the last two guests to arrive, and then paused the recording when they turned up at the door. She zoomed in to focus on Molly's image. The pictures pinned to a mirror in Molly's bedroom matched the frozen image. She'd reviewed the names on the list earlier in the investigation, but she hadn't made the connection until now. Molly's mum was in a relationship with Finch.

Karen's mind somersaulted as it worked hard to make the connections. She flicked through the file and pulled out the witness statements. She found Molly's and read through it.

The account of the evening and the altercation mirrored all the other statements they had gathered. Karen searched out Harry Coleman's statement. It too offered nothing new or revealing. But Karen considered whether Molly's unknown whereabouts would lead her to Harry. It was the most plausible option if she needed a place to stay.

A further check on Molly Brennan revealed several occasions where social services and police had been called. Angie Brennan had been cautioned twice for being drunk and disorderly and cautioned once for being in possession of a class B substance. At the time, Angie had sworn it wasn't hers. Knowing what she knew now, Karen didn't doubt that.

Molly had experienced a fractured and unstable home life. No wonder she hadn't been there when they'd raided the apartment.

Karen moved over to her screen and watched a different video feed. She wondered if Molly had been home the night Taylor had been murdered. Had she seen Finch heading out? Had she overheard him saying anything that would contradict his movements? Karen didn't view Molly as a suspect and nothing in her background suggested any violent tendencies.

The Copthorne estate images filled her screen. Residents milled around, the lights from the odd car peppered the darkness and then disappeared from view. Still nothing. The familiar images of Finch's gang appeared briefly near the playground, until they too wandered off. Karen paused the video and took a break. Her eyes ached, her back was stiff and her shoulders felt tight. She fetched a bottle of water from the kitchen and made her way back to her office, via the main floor. Steve and Brad were out making further enquiries, and Jade was ensconced in her workstation, but popped her head up when she saw Karen.

"Boss, I've seen a report from Essex Police. They've fished out a body from the River Chelmer near Little Baddow last night. He's been ID'd as Joel Adams. The report states gunshot wound to the head. His wrists and ankles were bound. He's got connections to our area, so their officers have contacted us for further information."

"Sounds like an execution?"

Jade agreed as she confirmed that Essex Police would conduct the investigations surrounding the grisly discovery and the Met would offer them any assistance they needed.

Alarm bells rang as Jade pulled up an image of the man and read the description. "Two-tone" Charlie had said that Adams had a dragon tattoo on his neck, and was at least six foot tall with a skull tattooed on one finger. The report filed by Essex Police and the images taken of the body confirmed her suspicions. It was the same person. *Someone was tying up loose ends.*

For the time being she needed to get back to her video analysis, but made a mental note to contact the SIO in Essex later. The ballistics report would interest her.

Karen sipped her water as she started the tape again. It was a while before the footage captured Molly Brennan leaving for the evening. She watched as Molly appeared from the side of an apartment block and made her way across the central square. She made her way to the car park on the other side. The image was darker as she zoomed in; there were fewer lights. Karen cursed as the image pixelated further. She could make out the outline of Molly as she stepped into a car.

The car remained stationary for a few minutes before it moved off and appeared on a closer feed. Karen identified the shape of a Saab. She jotted down the index of the car before running a check on it. The registered keeper of a red Saab 93 was Harry Coleman.

Karen let the tape run as she contemplated the new information. During the night someone had used the gun in Finch's possession. Had Molly lent the gun to anyone? Had she even seen it? Karen couldn't be certain of either.

At no point had Karen seen evidence of a firearm when she observed Finch and his gang. The timestamp on the tape showed two thirteen a.m. when the same Saab returned. Molly exited the car and headed back to the apartment, but Karen noticed that the Saab didn't pull away, nor did the driver leave the car.

"Who are you waiting for?" she mumbled.

Karen checked the timestamp again and it was two twenty-eight a.m. when a figure appeared from the apartment block. Karen recognised Molly, but this time she was half walking/half running towards the car.

Karen's eyes were glued to the screen, a mixture of concern and curiosity keeping her transfixed.

Had something happened in the apartment? Had the girl seen something that made her flee?

Karen noticed her carrying a Sainsbury's bag. Molly made her way to the Saab, and returned a few minutes later without the bag.

Karen watched the tail lights of the Saab disappear into the darkness.

42

"WHAT ARE WE LOOKING FOR, BOSS?" Jade asked as she walked with Karen to a smaller office containing a few PC terminals linked into the online archive database.

"We're looking for anything around Macholl. His life, his crimes, and any intelligence gathered on him."

Recently, the searching and analysing of past crimes had become automated as more records were transferred online.

It meant storage rooms had become redundant, and their contents shipped off to third-party storage facilities, or scanned and put on to online databases.

"I still can't see the connection between Molly, Taylor and Macholl?" Jade commented.

Karen had to confess she didn't know, either. She wondered if Molly had been convinced to pass a gun to a person unknown.

Had she done it under duress? Had she been intimidated, blackmailed or bribed? Or had she been a willing accessory to a double murder?

Only Molly could answer that, and the need to locate her became even more pressing.

Jade searched the database by using the keywords, "Dean Macholl." Her search pulled up forty-three reference points relating to his name.

"He's been a busy boy," Karen muttered as she scanned the list. Each line listed his name with an opening sentence relating to each reference point. The entry relating to the Paddy Power botched raid grabbed her attention, and she instructed Jade to open that entry.

They spent the next hour reviewing all the witness statements hoping something would jump out at them. Despite the third robber being potentially identified as Finch, nothing in the records threw up anything concrete. At the time, investigating officers had interviewed Finch as a suspect, but released him due to insufficient evidence. She wondered if Finch had plotted his revenge, but orchestrated the recent raid on the convenience store to give him a cast-iron alibi while another associate committed the murders?

"Boss, if Finch didn't get his share at the time, then maybe he waited for Macholl to return, confronted each of them, and when neither coughed up, he shot them?"

"That's possible, Jade. If that's the case, then we are looking for another suspect not on our radar."

When no new information was forthcoming, Karen resigned herself to accepting she wasn't going to get her answers searching through the archives.

Karen sensed that lazy afternoon feeling amongst the team as they gathered after lunch. Her immediate team of Jade, Steve and Brad sat to one side of her as the majority of the MIT fanned out around her perching on desks, or squatting on the nearest chairs. More than two dozen police officers and support staff waited as she finished making notes on the incident board.

"Listen, I know we are all tired. We've been working on this case for over a week now, and just as we think we're getting closer, something gets in the way and screws it up."

There were nods from those who had gathered.

"Boss, I think what's pissing us off is a lack of motive. We've got all these random players, and we've followed up leads and found nothing but dead ends."

Karen understood the frustration and sympathised with them. She reassured them she felt just the same.

"The motive has always been an issue for us. And perhaps that's why we have made little progress."

To clarify, Karen elaborated. "We've been focusing on recent events and focusing on connections. There is a historical element to this. And we were looking at suspects involved in criminality. I went back over the tapes the night that Taylor was murdered. I reviewed footage of the restaurant, and of the Copthorne estate. I compared the two."

Karen turned and pinned up still images she had printed off from the video footage. They were pictures of Molly exiting the red Saab after the dinner party and then returning to it minutes later.

"Molly Brennan?" an officer piped up from the back.

Karen nodded, and went on to explain the time between Molly arriving back at the apartment empty-handed, and then returning fifteen minutes later with a Sainsbury's carrier bag which she passed on to the driver of the Saab.

"My initial theory was that Finch used the handgun to shoot Taylor. But he has an alibi. He was doing over the convenience store. So as it stands, he's out of the equation."

"Do you have a new theory then?" someone asked.

Karen tapped the image of Molly Brennan. "I'm assuming that Molly knew about Finch's handgun and sneaked it out to her boyfriend, Harry Coleman or someone driving his car."

"So do you think maybe Harry Coleman shot Taylor?"

"I don't think Molly did. I think she passed the handgun to Harry. Whether or not he shot Taylor is a different matter. He may have passed it on to someone else who committed the act."

Brad crossed his arms and looked perplexed. His beady, piercing eyes fixed wide, staring at Karen. "I don't get it, boss. What's the motive? I can't see how she's connected to Taylor or Macholl. She's only seventeen, and when Macholl did a runner, she would have been eleven."

Brad had a point, but it was the only solid and tangible lead she had to go on. "As I said earlier, Brad, there has to be a historical element to this. It's just out of our grasp at the moment, but we need to bring Molly in."

"Where is she?" Brad continued. "We know she lived with her mum, but she's not been seen. And frankly I don't blame her. The apartment was a shithole."

Karen nodded and turned to address the whole team. "We know Molly is vulnerable. The estate will be the last place she seeks refuge. I believe she is with Harry Coleman. She's young and impressionable. And the chances are, she feels safe around him."

"Neither Molly nor Harry have form, boss. Not even a caution. They're both clean," Steve offered.

"There's always a first time. Find Harry, we find Molly?" Brad surmised.

Karen nodded, and she knew where to start.

43

Eric Street in Mile End was a narrow street with small, terraced housing to one side where front doors tipped out on to the narrow pavements. On the opposite side were low-level apartment blocks, a combination of privately owned and council-run properties.

Jade drove up and down the street a few times until they found the address in question, a grey and white block three stories high. Purple wheelie bins lined the pathways leading up to the apartments. They stood out as bright colourful beacons in the dreariness that surrounded them.

Karen glanced up and noticed that many of the apartments had their lights on. People had returned home, and were no doubt making dinner, or getting on with family life. Number fifty-four, however, sat in darkness as Karen peered through the ground-floor window. There appeared to be no signs of life, which Jade confirmed as she crouched and peered through the letter box, listening for sounds.

Jade hammered on the door a few times before stepping back and joining Karen on the pavement. Karen checked up and down the street and couldn't see a red Saab 93.

"They could be out cruising the streets or hanging out with friends," Jade offered.

"Or, they knew we would knock on their door soon."

Karen was determined to return a few hours later, but in the meantime, she instructed the team to continue trawling through CCTV footage surrounding Taylor's property and Macholl's apartment.

The team pushed on, and to keep going they ordered in a large Chinese delivery. Before long, the incident room filled with the blended spices and aromas of chow mein, fried rice, chicken and black bean sauce, and various other delights. Officers ate at their workstations, flicking through different video clips between each mouthful. Extended hours were a hazard of the job. It messed with home lives, plans were often put on hold, kids would miss their mummy or daddy reading them a bedtime story, and personal relationships became strained to breaking point.

The team took it in turns to review footage, so nothing was missed. It wasn't glamorous. It was time-consuming. Eyes hurt, shoulders ached, and minds played tricks as the hours ticked by.

Karen and Jade shared a terminal together as they looked at some footage close to where Taylor lived. Brad and Steve did the same but with Macholl's apartment.

"I hope you didn't have any plans tonight?" Karen asked Jade.

Jade shook her head. "I wish I did. But I'm useless at planning. I always end up cancelling meals and dates."

Karen raised a teasing brow. "Dates?"

Jade blushed. "I'm not a nun you know, boss. Believe it or not, I try to have a life outside of work… sometimes."

They both laughed, commiserating over the complete lack of work-life balance.

"So, is there a man in your life? I remember you were seeing someone a few months ago? Greg something or other?"

Jade winked. "No, boss. And it wasn't Greg; it was George. I'm keeping my options open. If a dashing young accountant wants to take me to dinner, then I won't be saying no. Quite the opposite. And I'm sure my parents would approve."

Jade's tone was prim and polite Karen thought, and in marked contrast to some around her who could barely string a sentence together.

"Oh my God!" Jade said as she paused the footage.

They were looking at footage from a property about two hundred yards from Taylor's. The CCTV camera covered the resident's front garden and some of the main road. For a fleeting second, Jade picked up a Saab 93 that slowed to a halt before moving off again. She zoomed in on the image and made out a partial index plate.

"The partial index matches the start of Harry Coleman's plate. I'd say that's more than just a coincidence, wouldn't you, boss?"

"I agree. It's the same car. I noticed the additional rear strip of brake lights flashing I saw on the Saab from the Copthorne state. Have you got any other footage from further down the road to help us identify where the car went?"

"No, boss. There are some other residential cameras further down that way, but the Saab isn't picked up and there are two turnings between where this camera is positioned and the next available footage. So, I guess the Saab pulled up."

Karen circled with her hand, urging Jade to continue running the footage. By now Steve had joined them and was perched over Karen's shoulder.

They watched in silence for the next few minutes until a lone figure in dark clothing walked past. Tension rippled amongst them like static electricity.

Karen checked the timestamp. The figure walked past at three eleven a.m. The odd car passed by in full view of the camera but there was nothing until three forty-four a.m. when what appeared to be the same figure darted past at speed headed in the opposite direction. A few more minutes passed before the Saab came into view and disappeared.

"The time frame fits, boss. Wainwright put the estimated time of death at between three and five a.m. Harry Coleman drives a Saab, and we presume he was in the car when he left Molly's less than an hour earlier. There's nothing else before the sighting that ties in with our case."

"That's all we need. We can pull in Harry Coleman in connection with the murder of Jack Taylor. If it wasn't him in the footage, then maybe he was the driver and we can find out who else was involved." Karen jumped up and out of her seat, ready to move. She instructed Brad to continue looking at all the footage around Macholl's apartment to see if a Saab had been in the vicinity.

Karen was relieved they hadn't encountered Coleman on their earlier visit. The lad posed a greater risk since he may have been involved with firearms and a murder. While the team busied themselves, Karen arranged for an arrest warrant and armed backup. After the events of the past, she was in no mood to take any risks.

"Boss, you should see this." Brad handed Karen a printout from background checks that support staff had been doing for him. It was a housing record from the council and a birth certificate.

Karen took a double take as she pored over the details. Number fifty-four Eric Street used to have a tenant called Elaine Atkins. Elaine Atkins had a son, Harry. Her eyes widened as she read the details of both parents on the birth certificate.

Karen's mind bubbled as she processed the connections and stared at Brad.

Brad nodded in return. "Harry changed his surname from Atkins to Coleman seven months ago. He's Elaine's son. And yes, you read the father's name correctly."

"Oh my god," Karen fumed as she rubbed her temples. "We didn't see that one."

THE DARKNESS ADDED an extra layer of animosity and intimidation to Eric Street as Karen and the other officers gathered. The street was empty, not a soul in sight. She could hear a dog barking somewhere in the distance in someone's back garden. Karen, Jade and Steve donned their stab jackets before two uniformed officers and two firearms officers joined them. The tactical entry team were positioned further down the road in case Karen needed them. She instructed Steve, a uniformed officer, and one firearms officer to cover the back of the block while the others went with her through the front door.

The next few minutes would make or break the case.

44

Karen and Steve exchanged updates over their radios as they positioned themselves. Karen knew they couldn't hang around, since it wouldn't take much for the heavy police presence to alert all the residents. They made their way towards the front door of fifty-four. Being a council property, the door was thin. Karen leant into the door to test its strength. A solid door would have required the tactical entry team, and she didn't have time for that.

Karen glanced at those gathered and gave the nod. The uniformed police officer with her was built like an ox, a little overweight, but his bulk provided an added advantage as he readied himself to kick the door in. The armed officer stood by with her Heckler shouldered, the Maglite torch attached to her weapon switched on and aimed at the door. She would be the first in, followed by the others.

Jade knocked on the door. There was no answer. She crouched and peered through the letter box to see the faint glimmer of a light towards the far end of the hallway. She could hear the TV from somewhere within the property.

Karen knocked again. When no answer was forthcoming, she stepped away from the door.

Karen keyed the radio. “Steve, we’re going in on a count of three.”

“Confirmed.”

Karen counted to three on her fingers before screaming, “Go, Go, Go!”

The heavy boot of the officer crashed into the door, but it didn’t cave in. He stepped back and launched at the door again. Cracks appeared in the frame, and the door creaked. On his third attempt, the door flung back and slammed against the wall, its latch surrendering.

“Police! Stay where you are!” the armed officer screamed as she tore down the hallway, glancing in each room as she made her way through. A solid pure beam of light cut right through the darkness as the armed officer waved her weapon in small arcs looking for any sign of movement.

Steve came over the radio. “Movement at the rear, movement at the rear.”

At that moment, the armed officer with Karen screamed instructions from a bedroom off to Karen’s left. “Move away from the bed, and get down on the floor, face down with your arms spread out in front of you! Do it now! Now!” the officer screamed.

Karen’s attention was drawn in different directions before she nodded towards the back room. Jade and a police officer rushed past her. Karen turned into the bedroom just as the armed officer switched on the light, her gun still trained on the shaking figure on the floor. The unmistakable long, dark brown hair, and slim figure belonged to Molly Brennan. She sobbed, her slight body quaking with fear.

"It's okay, Molly. We are not here to hurt you. Are there firearms in this premises that we need to be made aware of?" Karen asked as she knelt over the girl and secured her arms behind her back with handcuffs.

There was a tremble in Molly's voice as she shook her head in small violent jerks. Her voice was soft and laced with fear. "No."

"Molly, I'm arresting you on suspicion of involvement in the murder of Jack Taylor and Dean Macholl. You do not have to say anything, but it may harm your defence if you do not mention when questioned something that you later rely on in court. Anything you do or say may be given in evidence. Do you understand?"

Molly lay in silence, shivering on the floor as if locked away in her own world.

"Molly, do you understand?" Karen repeated.

"Yes," came a timid reply.

Karen nodded at the firearms officer to remain in the room as she rose to her feet and rushed through to the lounge at the rear of the apartment. She joined Jade who peered out of a large open window that looked out across a row of gardens that spanned across the back of the apartments. The other uniformed officer had already raced back out of the apartment to join the chase to apprehend the other suspect.

Together, Karen and Jade watched as Steve and the officers tracked down the fugitive who they hoped was Harry Coleman. The light from torches darted back and forth in jerky movements as the officers raced through the gardens and back alleyways.

Fearing the suspect might get away, Karen reached for her radio in readiness to call for backup but paused when Steve came over the airwaves. "Suspect detained. I repeat suspect detained." His message came through as the sound of screams, commands and raised voices echoed through the darkness.

Karen keyed her radio. "Steve, can you confirm it's Harry Coleman?" A few seconds of silence followed, but in Karen's mind it felt like minutes as she waited for a positive ID. She glanced at Jade, and noticed the same concern etched on her face as she narrowed her eyes and stared out into the darkness beyond the window.

Karen's radio crackled into life. "Yes, boss. I can confirm we have detained Harry Coleman."

"Yes!" Karen punched the air. "Well done, Steve. Can you bring him back here?"

"That's a good result, boss."

Karen nodded and agreed. "Jade, can you organise SOCO to attend? We need to put these two in paper suits and secure all their clothing for forensic analysis. With luck, we'll find gunshot residue on something belonging to Harry Coleman, and perhaps even Molly."

Jade wandered off as she contacted the control room to organise extra resources.

"Oh, and Jade, stand down the tactical team!" Karen shouted as she snapped on a pair of blue latex gloves.

Jade waved her hand over her shoulder in acknowledgement as she walked through the hallway.

Now that the scene was secure, Karen could take in the apartment for the first time. It wasn't the worst she'd seen, but from its appearance, it hadn't been maintained recently and lacked a bit of TLC. The sofas had seen better days. Large indentations marked out where occupants had sat over the years. There was a free-standing shelf unit in one corner, featuring pictures dating back over the years of Harry at different ages. Karen paused at a few showing him in school uniform, grinning with delight into the camera lens. Karen thought that he looked happy, a child untainted by the harshness of life. There were other photos of Harry alongside a woman which she assumed was his mum. The woman had an arm wrapped around him, poised with her lips against his cheek much to his embarrassed, scrunched-up face.

The snapshots depicted happy days, but she felt a tinge of sadness as she wondered how happiness had turned to sorrow, and what Harry must have experienced after the death of his mother. He must have felt alone and abandoned. *God knows what must have been going through his mind at the time.*

The rest of the apartment had a similar undertone. A warm, family home neglected in recent years. Both bedrooms were tidy but not clean. Karen wandered through the kitchen which was basic and functional. She noticed that the plates had been washed and sat on the plate dryer beside the sink. She raised an eyebrow and nodded in approval. The work surfaces were free of clutter, and she cast an eye over the row of cereal packets. Cornflakes, cheap own-brand rice crispies, and Coco Pops neatly stacked towards the far end of the counter.

No wonder Molly escaped here. Karen thought back to the state of Angie Brennan's apartment. Harry's apartment felt like a palace in comparison.

45

No firearms were discovered at fifty-four Eric Street, and as a result, firearms officers were stood down. Forensic officers spent most of the night going over the property with a fine-tooth comb. Items of clothing belonging to both Molly Brennan and Harry Coleman were secured as potential evidence.

For the first time in over a week, Karen slept peacefully without the help of alcohol or a one-night stand with a random stranger. Harry Coleman had been detained in the cells overnight, and because of Molly's age and her mum in hospital, social services had taken her into care before returning with her this morning.

"How are you going to play this, boss?" Jade asked as she stood over Karen's shoulder. They watched the monitors of the interview suites holding Harry Coleman and Molly Brennan.

"We'll speak to Molly first," Karen replied. She scrutinised Molly's movements in the interview suite. The young girl pulled her shoulders closer into her chest and looked around, chewing on her bottom lip. She looked frightened and nervous. A social worker from the local council had been appointed to support and assist Molly. Their presence made sure that Molly understood her rights and ensured that the police treated her fairly and properly while being interviewed. "Any news from forensics?"

"Not yet, boss. I chased them about thirty minutes ago. They promised to have preliminary results for us in the next hour or so."

Karen huffed and hoped that would be the case. It was another reason why she'd decided to interview Molly first. Between the pair, Molly was the weakest link, and more likely to give up information than Harry. It would buy time, so she had more evidence to present to Harry when she interviewed him.

As Karen and Jade stepped through to the interview room, Molly's eyes widened, and her lips tightened into a thin line as she sat bolt upright. The social worker, a thin lady with a soft smile, placed a reassuring hand on Molly's arm.

Karen began by explaining the reason for the interview and announcing those present in thc room for the benefit of the recorder.

"Molly, to help our investigations could you answer some questions for us?" Karen's voice was soft but firm. She needed Molly's full cooperation, but equally, she needed to create a rapport that didn't intimidate the young girl.

Molly nodded.

Karen told Molly to verbalise all her questions and answers for the benefit of the tape recorder.

"Molly, can you tell us how long you've been in a relationship with Harry Coleman?"

Molly stumbled and stuttered with her words, which were soft and timid. "Um… hmmm… just over a year I guess."

"And how long has Darren Finch been staying at your mother's apartment?"

Molly shrugged her shoulders. "I'm not sure, to be honest. It seems like ages."

Karen sensed a cracking in Molly's voice at the mere mention of Darren Finch. She explored the angle further, and Molly eventually opened up about how domineering and controlling Finch had been with her mum. And how her mum had been a soft target for Finch and his gang. The true horrors of Angie Brennan's relationship with Finch began to unfold as Molly's voice quivered, and her eyes moistened as she revealed details of the abuse her mum had suffered at his hands.

Karen and Jade exchanged glances when Molly revealed Finch had got her mum so high on drugs that Finch, along with his thugs, had gang-raped her to ensure compliance.

"And where were you when this was happening, Molly?" Karen probed.

"Finch shut me in my bedroom and told me not to come out unless I wanted the same." Molly glanced down at the table. She squeezed her eyes, and the first tears dropped on to the table.

The social worker squeezed Molly's arm and rubbed her back.

"Molly, are you okay to continue?" Karen asked.

"Yes."

Karen let the silence sit between them. She was in no hurry to push Molly and wanted Molly to continue at her own pace.

"I hated Finch. Things were just about okay with me and my mum. Then Finch came along and ruined everything. I just wanted to be out of there whenever I knew Finch was going to turn up. He would touch me."

Karen and Jade focused. Jade scribbled down a few notes.

Karen probed further around that last point. Molly revealed how he would come into her bedroom and touch her inappropriately, or when she was in the kitchen trying to find something to eat, he would come in and shut the door behind him. Molly shuddered as she recalled how he would pin her up against the work surface from behind and thrust his groin into her backside, saying how he was going to ruin her. She told Karen about being trapped and groped in the stairwell, if she was unfortunate enough to bump into him.

Karen reminded Molly how brave she was. Further details about the sexual assaults only confirmed that they would have additional evidence to use against Finch. Karen felt angry and disgusted with Finch's behaviour. He had not only preyed on the vulnerable but had preyed on the young. Molly was still a minor, and he had intimidated and conditioned her as a precursor to his vile plans.

Karen wanted to shake her head in frustration and sadness but held back. The depravity she came across in her job left her feeling helpless.

"I knew about his gun and the drugs, so when I told Harry about the stuff we'd been going through, he said he had an idea of how to get Finch out of my life once and for all. I didn't know what he meant, and I didn't want to know. I wanted this to all end." Molly stared at Karen through bloodshot eyes, her eyelids red and sore. "I wanted to be… happy. And Harry made me happy. For the first time in my life I felt loved and wanted. There was no catch with Harry. He wanted to care for me. Harry promised that everything would be okay, and that the people who had hurt me and him would never get the chance to do that again." Her voice petered out.

Molly confirmed that she had given the gun to Harry, and that he had returned it. She also revealed that Finch kept a sizeable amount of cash and drugs in the storeroom of a local café. Molly had followed him one day and had found him round the back of the café, screwing a waitress up against the wall. She added it wasn't the last time, either.

Karen nodded at Jade who excused herself from the interview room for a few moments while she organised for officers to visit the café to search for the evidence. Once Jade was back in the suite, Karen continued the interview.

Karen went through Molly's statement again, asking further questions. She found no evidence to link her to Taylor or Macholl other than through Harry. Molly's desperate plight touched Karen. She was young and naïve, a victim of coercion and abuse. A troubled and broken home life left her vulnerable.

Molly glanced between the two officers, searching for anything in their faces that would help her understand what would happen next.

“What will happen to Harry?” she asked.

“We don’t know yet. We are still to interview him,” Karen replied.

“Harry is no different. He’s just as sad and as lonely as me. That’s why we got on so well. We needed each other. Can I wait for him?”

Karen didn’t have the heart to tell her it was unlikely that Harry would be released.

“I don’t think that would be a good idea. We don’t know how long we’ll be. It’s not very comfortable here, so I suggest that you go back with this lovely lady who’s looking after you, and we will be in touch with you very soon.”

46

After doing the introductions and caution for the tape, Karen took a few moments to study Harry Coleman. He was tall, well built, with full lips and a strong, chiselled jawline. He had a constant scowl etched on his face, and despite that, still bore evidence of being a young adult with an acne-ridden forehead. He didn't display the same nervousness she had witnessed in Molly. He appeared more relaxed with his back pushed into the chair, and his hands resting on the table with his fingers interlocked. There were no signs of a tremor in his fingers.

It had been two hours since Karen and Jade had interviewed Molly. They'd taken a break in between the interviews to compare notes, and to gather as much evidence as possible before starting their interview with Harry. The wait had paid off as they sat across the table from Harry and a duty solicitor, appointed upon his request. His eyes flicked between the two female officers, but again Karen sensed no nervousness in his demeanour.

Harry remained calm. Too calm.

"Harry, how well did you know Jack Taylor?"

"Not very well. I hadn't spoken to him much. He hardly gave me the time of day when I went round there to see Ben. Whatever I heard, Ben told me."

"What did Ben tell you?" Karen probed.

"How much he hated him. What a bastard he was to his mum."

"Did Ben tell you about Jack assaulting him?"

Harry shrugged a shoulder. "Maybe."

"He did, or he didn't. Which is it?"

Harry cleared his throat and licked his dry lips. He paused for a second to take a sip from the styrene cup of tea. "Yes, he did. He told me that Jack had beaten him a couple of times. Even though Ben hadn't provoked him other than to protect his mum, Jack beat the crap out of him and smacked him in the mouth a couple of times."

"So did Ben at any time ask you to seek revenge on his behalf?"

Harry shook his head. "No."

Karen changed direction. "How much contact did you have with Dean Macholl?"

"Not much. He's not been around for the last six years."

"And before that?"

"I used to see him around. He used to come and see Mum quite a lot, and then when she got together with Jack, he stopped contact."

"When did you find out that Dean Macholl was your father and Ben was your half-brother?"

"Ages ago. And that's why I had to protect Ben."

"Does Ben know about it?"

"No."

"So, you couldn't stand by and see your half-brother being used as a punchbag."

Harry nodded. "Ben wasn't brave enough to fight back. Jack was making his life a misery."

Karen started revealing some information they had just received from forensic analysis. "The gun we recovered from Molly's apartment has your partial fingerprints on it. It's the same gun used to shoot Jack Taylor and Dean Macholl. We also have CCTV footage that places your car in the vicinity of Jack Taylor's house around the time someone killed him. Were you responsible for shooting Jack Taylor and Dean Macholl?"

There was an uncomfortable silence as Harry studied the faces of those around the table.

"No."

"Are you sure about that? Because your car was picked up less than two hundred yards away from Dean Macholl's apartment on the night he was killed. Now I don't believe in coincidences. I put it to you, Molly Brennan sneaked out the handgun and passed it to you on both occasions." Karen slid across the table still images of Molly exiting Harry's car empty-handed on the night that Taylor was shot dead before returning fifteen minutes later carrying something. "You shot both victims and then returned the gun to her."

"No comment."

Karen sighed. She hated when suspects ventured down the "no comment" route. But she had to keep pushing.

"Do you blame Jack Taylor for your mum's death?"

Harry's eyelids twitched. She had touched on a raw nerve. And despite his calm exterior, his emotions boiled just beneath the surface. He tried to relax his hands, but an involuntary force inside him curled his fingers into tight-fisted balls. Karen spotted the change in his body language as his shoulders tightened, and his jawbones flexed.

"After all, it was Jack Taylor who pulled the trigger, and your mum died because of it. I guess anyone in your position would naturally feel angry and revengeful?"

A groan rumbled deep within Harry's throat, before he tapped the side of his fist on the tabletop.

"Come on, let's make this easier for all of us. We can keep you here for twenty-four hours and then apply for an extension. But the evidence is stacking up against you."

Harry wasn't budging.

"There's gunshot residue on the items of clothing we recovered from your flat. It's a match for the handgun retrieved."

"That doesn't mean they're my clothes."

Karen smiled. "Hair fibres and particles of skin we recovered from *inside* the clothes are a DNA match for you. So, we have your partial prints on the gun. We have your car in the vicinity at the time both men were murdered, and we have gunshot residue on the clothes we recovered from your flat. That's more than enough to charge you with homicide."

A knock sounded at the door. Brad popped his head in and beckoned Karen outside. Reluctantly Karen paused the interview and stepped out into the corridor.

"This better be good, Brad. Coleman was just about to crack. I know it."

Brad looked confused. "Sorry, boss. You said you wanted to know as soon as the search had been conducted at the café?"

Karen shook her head and ran her fingers through her hair. "Sorry. Sorry. Yes, you're right. My mistake. What have you got?"

"I've just heard back from the officers. They found a box with a sizeable amount of cash stashed at the back of the freezer. There is at least a couple of grand there. Also, several large bags of what they believe to be amphetamines. They'll be sent away for analysis, but it's probably something like ecstasy or MDMA."

Buoyed by the results, Karen re-joined the interview and continued where she'd left off.

"You see, I think this has all been about revenge. Taylor killed your mum. Whether that was intentional or an accident, he's still responsible for pulling the trigger that led to your mum's death. And Dean abandoned you and your mother when Jack came on the scene. You both weren't worth fighting for in his eyes? So, I think this is about settling scores. Am I correct?"

Harry slammed his fist on the table again. He was falling apart at the seams, his cool exterior showing the first signs of cracks. "They killed my mum! And they have never shown a day of remorse. They used her, like they used everyone. They had to pay the price. Taylor and Dean took away the only thing I had in my life, my mum. Why should they get away with it?"

"Did you kill Jack Taylor?"

Harry nodded. "Yes." Malice and hatred coloured his tone as he spat the word out. "I killed the bastard. And I would do it again, if I had the chance. I've got nothing to live for, and I've got nothing to lose."

"What about Molly?" Karen asked. "Doesn't she mean anything to you? Do you not think she's been through enough already?"

Harry fell silent for a few moments as he stared into nothingness beyond Karen.

Karen pushed further. "If Taylor used your mum, did you use Molly?"

Harry sneered at Karen. "No, of course she means something to me. I couldn't have done this without her?"

"That doesn't sound like someone in love with her. You pulled her into your plot for revenge which has now made her an accessory to the murder of two men."

"I was trying to make her life easy. We're surrounded by dickheads. By using Finch's gun, we could drop him in it and get him out of her life for good. She was all up for that."

Karen reflected for a few moments. It was hard to tell whether Harry had used Molly for his own gains, or whether they had naïvely concocted some kind of Bonnie and Clyde scenario in their minds.

"And why did you shoot Dean Macholl?"

"He was just as much to blame for my mum's death as Taylor. Dean was a coward. He promised my mum he would always protect her and me. But he didn't stop Taylor from shooting my mum. Taylor pulled the trigger, but Dean was just as guilty. As soon as my mum ended up with Taylor, Dean forgot about us. It's almost like he… gave up on us."

Karen sat back in her chair. She'd got the confession.

"I never got the chance to say goodbye to her," Harry whispered.

47

THE TEAM GATHERED around the incident board for a final debrief. A feeling of excitement and relief rippled amongst the whole team as over twenty officers and support staff grabbed any free space to sit or perch.

"Well done, team. We've got a great result." Karen started off her speech, beaming with a big smile. "Two murder cases solved, a handgun off the street, over ten thousand pounds in cash seized, and probably the same amount again in drugs."

A collective round of applause rang out as the team congratulated each other.

"We've also got Finch charged with possession of firearms and drugs. More importantly, we've also charged him with a range of sexual offences against both an adult and a minor."

"That's one less perv roaming the streets," someone muttered from the back of the crowd.

The comment was met with several nodding heads and mutterings.

"Absolutely. He was forcefully grooming Molly Brennan and had we not arrested him as part of our investigations, then I suspect Molly's fate would have turned out a lot worse."

Karen wrapped up the final few pieces and confirmed the sequence of events. The long task of preparing the case lay ahead even though Harry Coleman would be appearing in front of the magistrates' first thing in the morning.

KAREN NOTICED the DCI lurking towards the back of the group while she did the debrief. He followed her into her office, and she groaned as he swung through the door.

"That was a good result, Karen. The team worked hard. My treat to a round of drinks down the road. Everyone seems in a good mood, so let's make the most of it. Well deserved, including you."

The last thing Karen wanted was to stand around in a pub and toast their success. Despite an impromptu celebration being good for team morale, she felt physically and mentally exhausted. Her head ached, and her eyes felt like they had sandbags attached to the lids. She didn't want to be considered a party pooper, but a glass of red wine, a hot soak in the bath and a little binge on Netflix seemed more appealing to her.

"I've got a few phone calls to make, sir, and then I'll join you."

KAREN FOUND the team squeezed into a corner of the pub. A collective cheer sounded around her as the DCI brought over a large tray of drinks and announced, "Sip these slowly, because it's the first and last drinks I'm going to buy you lot."

His instruction was met with a round of jeers as a clamour of hands reached across the tray. Karen had opted for a gin and tonic and enjoyed the light taste as it trickled and hit the spot. She closed her eyes and enjoyed the feeling of stress melt from her shoulders.

"You look shattered, boss," Jade remarked as she nudged Karen in the arm.

Karen rolled her eyes. "I think that's an understatement. I could go to sleep now and not wake up for two days. I can't be arsed with the thought of getting on the Tube and heading home. If only we could click our fingers and teleport our bodies in a matter of seconds. I would pay good money for that." She laughed.

Jade agreed as she took a large gulp from her wine glass. "I would say we could grab a bite to eat on the way home and you can crash at mine, but I'm meeting someone."

Karen waved it off with her hand. The noise in the pub grew louder as more people arrived. And with the surrounding din, she found it hard to hear what Jade was saying. "Don't be daft. I think if I sat down to eat, I'd fall asleep sitting up."

She wondered how many of the team really wanted to be here and she looked around. Many were married to their jobs and probably saw each other more than they saw their own partners at home. That didn't matter as much for the single Karen, but she pondered how people maintained a healthy relationship. There was a high divorce rate in the emergency services, and many of her colleagues ended up single or having relationships with one another because their colleagues were the only ones who understood the pressures of the job.

Steve joined Karen and Jade. They talked amongst themselves and bet who would be the first amongst the crowd to leave. They agreed it would be Brad. He was often the odd one out. He was socially awkward at times, and his piercing eyes stood out on stalks when he had a drink.

Twenty minutes later and on cue, the three of them noticed Brad surreptitiously slide his empty beer bottle across the bar and disappear back into the crowd before appearing towards the back. He circumnavigated the whole group to leave the pub from the furthest entrance.

"Who's the lucky lady tonight?" Karen asked Steve.

Steve's brow furrowed in reply.

Karen wafted her hand back and forth in front of her nose. "I can smell your aftershave from here. Anita? Tara? Or that waitress from the Jamaican restaurant. I can't recall her name but the one you introduced with the big…"

"Boss!" Jade interrupted with a squeal.

Karen's eyes lit up. "Let me finish. With the big… curly, long Afro ringlets." Karen clicked her fingers as she tried to remember.

Jade couldn't help but laugh.

"Jacinta. You're thinking of Jacinta."

"That's the one. I knew she had an exotic name. We liked her."

"No, she's just a friend."

"With benefits?" Jade chipped in with a wink.

Nothing that either Karen or Jade said unnerved Steve. He always had a cool and natural confidence around them.

"Meeting a lovely lady called Kaz. A personal trainer. I've only just met her. Well, actually I bumped into her in the doorway of the local Tesco's. We chatted, and I asked for her number."

"Smooth," Jade teased.

Karen shook her head. Steve had a natural magnetism that made women swoon over him.

Jade and Steve left, leaving Karen to say her final goodbyes to the rest of the team before making her excuses. She looked around for the DCI but couldn't find him, so she slipped out of the front door only to bump into him standing outside having a cigarette.

"Bollocks," she muttered under her breath.

"Karen, you're leaving the party already?"

"Um… yes, sir."

Skelton offered to buy her another drink which she politely declined. They stood there in silence for a few moments, the awkwardness rising between them as each second ticked by.

Karen shifted uncomfortably on the spot and then glanced at her phone. She looked around the street. In fact, she would rather be looking at a dripping tap than being stood by the DCI. "I really must shift, sir. I'm tired and have a long train ride home."

"Suit yourself," Skelton replied, dropping his cigarette butt on the floor and crushing it with the sole of his shoe.

She waited for him to disappear inside the pub before she blew out her cheeks with a sigh of relief. Melancholy swept over her. It felt like everyone had someone to see or somewhere to go but she found herself alone once again. A part of her didn't enjoy that feeling but she buried it rather than do something about it. One call she had made earlier had confirmed her suspicions and concerns. "Two-tone" Charlie hadn't been seen in the last twenty-four hours and his chip shop hadn't opened for business. It would be a waiting game now, but she'd make some discreet enquiries when she had the opportunity.

But tonight, she had somewhere else that she wanted to be. She crossed the road and walked until she saw the familiar orange glow of a taxi for hire sign looming in the distance. She flagged the vehicle down and stepped into the back.

The driver in the darkened cab looked over his shoulder. "Where to, luv?"

"Broomfield Residential Care Home, please."

NEXT IN THE SERIES – HIS LAST BREATH

CURRENT BOOK LIST

Hop over to my website for a current list of books:

http://jaynadal.com/current-books/

Printed in Dunstable, United Kingdom

67146173R00180